Siesta

(Concerning Anna)

By

Sally Campbell

This book is dedicated to

My Precious Three.

©Sally Campbell 2012

Facebook Group "**Sally Campbell - Author**"

Sally Campbell has asserted her rights under the Copyright, Designs and Patents Act of 1988 to be identified as the author of this work.

This Novel is entirely a work of fiction. Any resemblance to any persons, living or dead, events or localities is entirely coincidental

Published by

Roddy Muspratt

All rights reserved.

Linsey —

Hope you enjoy
This —

lots of love

to you

Sally x

Sept - 2013

Table of Contents

Siesta

The Man Who Danced with a Pig

The Prologue

About Sally Campbell.

Concerning Anna

'When do people actually take up gardening?' asked Victoria.

'When they give up sex of course – it offers the perfect replacement.' Anna took the question seriously – she loved any issue that was concerned with human behaviour.

'Horticultural Replacement Therapy?' offered Smiley. Her sunburnt face danced with amusement.

'You could say that,' confirmed Anna. Without humour. 'It's more peaceful – and a darn sight less messy.'

'Non-invasive pleasure,' said Victoria. 'Isn't manure just as messy – in a different way, of course?' Her clever narrow face matched her professional lawyer's tone. It was hard to tell when she was being serious or playful.

'Ha-ha,' from an impatient Honor. 'We aren't there yet, surely. None of us at this table – we're all under fifty. Gerald and I . . .' She broke off abruptly and a faint blush crept over her fine neglected cheekbones. Her three friends stared at her, waiting, while the waitress brought bowls of soup and bread.

'Enjoy.' She said this every week to them much to Victoria's irritation.

'Well?' said Smiley.

'We absolutely hate gardening,' said Honor, rather lamely.

'Really?' from Victoria. 'Didn't he give you a watering-can last Christmas and some bloody book on borders?'

'Well . . . yes. But you can't count that. I haven't opened the book once and the can is for the bird bath.' Everyone laughed at Honor's stammering explanation. And more when she said,

'We are starting a little vegetable patch – lettuces and that sort of thing. But no more than that.' She grabbed her bread roll, feeling suddenly horribly exposed. Her bedroom door wide open. She lying there – awake – with Gerald snoring by her side.

'Organic veggies, ay?' Smiley snorted. 'Vegetables of the organ – hm. It has a sort of familiar ring to it. I'm such a city person that the soil for me holds no charm whatsoever. Besides I absolutely hate bending over – always have.'

Victoria narrowed her indigo eyes – leant towards her and said 'But you do admit to a deep-seated and I mean deep-seated love of sex?'

'Not a fair question or assumption.' Anna's tone was emphatic and held no laughter – it rarely did these days.

'Smiley is the only one of us not married. She is exempt.'

'Oh, so it's only us?' Honor had quite regained her composure and was relieved to be sidelined. 'We count because of this.' She held up her left hand.

'That's right.' Anna nodded. Her tired intelligent face displaying a quiet interest in the subject.

'Poor old celibate us then. What is left for us but seeds, bulbs, perennials, compost, alkaline, deciduous, herbaceous, rambling, hanging, weeping, creeping and . . .'

'For a non-gardener you seem to have quite a vocabulary.' This, of course, from Victoria. 'I therefore pronounce you guilty of celibacy.'

'Rubbish! Look at my hands.' Honor spread creamy spiders before her on the table. 'Well, what do you think?'

'Hm,' was the general opinion. Even Victoria could think of nothing. It was clear they had never touched a tool – at least not the ones inferred just then

'Anna's hands! Your turn – come on. Sur la table.'

'Oh do I have to? This is awful. I'm ashamed to own two such things.' But she complied beneath silent inspection.

'Oh you poor love.' Smiley was the first to offer commiserations.

'Shocking!' from Honor – glad once again the attention was no longer on her.

'Self-evident,' declared Victoria – and the hands were quietly withdrawn and put away.

'Well,' said Anna, 'hands reflect a life – Johnny and I are broke. There's absolutely no point in hiding the fact. I work myself to the bone, I don't mind admitting it – and I love it. And if I look a worn out wreck – and I know I do – I don't give a fig.'

'You should though.' Victoria thought this but did not say so. She knew how desperate their financial situation was and had been for some time. But Johnny was an attractive man.

'Not fair on him though.' from Smiley, cautiously. From Honor too in silent half-hearted agreement.

'Why not?' Anna's voice sharpened. 'We've been married for twenty five years for God's sake. Be realistic – we are.'

'So?' All three said this, chiming in together.

'So? So, he knows me inside out. We don't need facades and designer clothes to get through our days. It's absurd and anyway I've never had time for that sort of rubbish'

'You should though,' Victoria thought again.

'Surely a bit of frivolity is important.' Smiley stated simply.

'Frivolity needs time – and money.' Anna told her shortly. 'Aren't other things more important – like loyalty, cheerfulness – being there?' They watched her – each holding on to their opinions.

'Johnny works so hard – do you honestly imagine he'd notice if I changed my hair, put on French knickers? No. But he'd notice if he didn't find a clean shirt in the cupboard. Food on the table. He'd notice a black rim round the bath. He has everything he needs and I can tell you it's worth ten bunk-ups or whatever they are called – or the latest lipstick.' She laughed then, and when Anna laughed her dormant prettiness shed twenty years bringing out her wild elfin looks. The three women were astonished by her. They all concluded the same. Here was a real woman – rare and selfless, confident enough to forsake vanity. Certain too of her place – she stood just behind him in support but was way ahead of him in wisdom. She embodied womanhood of the most perfect kind.

Smiley groaned inwardly – marriage was not for her. Ultimately women became like nurses to their men. As bodies deteriorated and lost their athletic charms, a wife's duty was then to keep it going for as long as possible – feed it, pet it, console it and listen to every sound that came from it. Duty did not allow even the faintest silent whisper of theoretical euthanasia to enter the by now exhausted mind. Stoic cheerfulness masked a multitude of ambivalent thoughts. It made Smiley flinch. Honor smiled guardedly to hide her own disquiet and Victoria nodded once. It wasn't clear whether this was out of impatience or agreement. The fact was that Anna had the unique ability to make people examine themselves.

She drove home slowly along lanes of cow parsley, the soft southern downs framing her vision. Had she enjoyed lunch? Had she been too serious? She hoped not.
But she did feel so weary these days – so old. It wasn't a bad feeling – it just made her speak her mind and yes, perhaps it made her seem intolerant – and boring. But women of our age often appear to have dull lives, she thought. Anna didn't see it like that. On the contrary, she loved being up against it – as long as the fight was worth it. She could endure anything. She would have loved the war and stayed to the bitter end. A cause!

Yes, of course she had enjoyed lunch. It had been so long since anyone had taken her anywhere. And she loved her friends, so different from one another. But now she was pleased to be alone again although she knew that to be alone was to worry. Company merely offered temporary relief. She preferred the raw reality. Worry was now her constant companion. Like a dog, a cat – a child. Always there. Although it did not need feeding it always needed attention. And in return it gave her insomnia, tense burning shoulders and fine lines all over her forty-seven year old face. Johnny never slept through a night. He'd wake at two, get up, go downstairs – read, watch television. From their room she'd hear him cough, move about. His anxiety rose through the ceiling, climbed into their bed and settled there. Silently she shared his sleepless hours in a dreaded anguish that enveloped her. Two hours generally. And then Johnny returned. She'd say nothing but to know he was beside her again filled her with relief. And somehow they'd manage to sleep before the alarm clock reminded them sharply of their ongoing problems.

Money of course. The lack of it. At the office always waiting for the big order. The one that would solve everything. Sometimes it would seem imminent. A foreign voice making solid enquiries, ringing back, making an appointment. Hope would tiptoe into the diary. How many times had that happened? And then the cancellation or perhaps not even that. The appointment simply not kept. Johnny loved his men and he looked after them. Like some sea captain, he steered their little boat crashing through forty-foot waves, desperately avoiding rocks. And he loved his wife. How could he not – the truest friend he had. Her abiding love, her faith in him. But rocks there were – everywhere.

'It will happen, Johnny. Keep going. It will be all right – you'll see. I know it will.' Blind faith. Stroking his hair.

'I love you, Johnny.'

Always the same – always there for him. He could see how tired she was – thin too – worn out by undeclared worry and her care of him. Her hands the image of their life. She had changed. The vitality had gone and taken with it the light that had perpetually danced in and around her eyes. And to the fore marching alongside him this selfless, steadfast person.

But no passion. No room for that. Too tired for that. Too familiar, too good a friend for that. Her skin, once the softest part of his day no longer felt his hands on it. His mind so immersed on crucial things could not recall desire – or the fulfilment it demanded. Her skin shed its velvet secret glow. They fell into passionless friendship bound together by the past. It made Johnny feel guilty. He had brought them to this

He watched her just then as she shelled the peas. With practised fingers she split open the pods and the peas fell into a bowl on the floor, held firm by her feet. Her old daisy-printed skirt draped easily over her separated legs. She was completely absorbed with the job. She stopped only to push imaginary hair away from her eyes. This she did with the back of her hand and she did it constantly. It was a new habit.

'Why do you keep doing that?' He asked.

'Doing what?' And she did it again. Johnny laughed. It made her look up at him. She loved to hear him laugh.

'That. Pushing hair that isn't there off your forehead.'

'Do I? How odd.' And back she went to her work. He continued to watch her. She had lovely hair. It was moon-coloured, shiny and young. In the early days he had found it incredibly exciting – irresistible – like burying his face in honeyed silver. She used to brush it in those days – one hundred long hard strokes – before bed. Now it was neat and practical – no longer seeking notice. Like some forgotten treasure whose glory lives boxed up.

Six thousand miles away in temperatures of forty centigrade and behind closed shutters, a man lay dying. He was not just any man. He lay in a magnificent brass bed, his head resting against lacy pillows. The women who surrounded him wore black. His wife, beautiful, dignified and just then immensely solemn, held his hand folded in both her own. She murmured to him; little words of comfort – of love – and he responded with a twitching smile. But he never opened his rich brown eyes. She knew that it was useless, that is why her daughters were there – and the priest. The young women, all married, cried softly. They hugged one another as they heard the priest say the last prayers – his voice was low and somewhat monotone. Isabel stared at her father's face; she could not believe that he no longer spoke. Neither did he move. Maria Marta could not look at him – death petrified her and to be now in the naked presence of this mystery made her feel faint. She thought she might fall. Her thin hand grasped the bed for support. Luz, the baby of the family, but now thirty-four years old comforted her sisters. She was not afraid. With coffee-pink lips she responded to the prayers. 'Espiritu Santo ……Espiritu Santo.' The sign of the cross. She released her sisters and they all kissed the crucifixes that hung from their necks. Don Juan Miguel Martinez Acevedo died peacefully at three o'clock in the afternoon. He was eighty-five and had led a good and privileged life. Buenos Aires mourned his passing. In drawing rooms everywhere about the city it was generally agreed that his unfailing good humour and remarkable gift for friendship were exceptional and would be sadly missed. He was a very rich man – both in land and money. He had loved his wife, adored his girls and he left them very well cared for. They each had a farm and astute investments besides.

And for the girl in England who he had not seen for many years but had never forgotten – he had left careful instructions. His lawyers were told to locate her on his death and inform her of his bequest. The professional men were surprised – so much? they asked. Who was this 'girl'? Incredible! Obviously some very discreet love interest – well, well. She was most likely married now. Her maiden name had been Forrester. The two lawyers winked at one another and set about finding her through their contacts in London.

The new widow allowed control to slip now. She embraced the dead man letting out an animal moan. Her daughters gathered closer and soon the room was consumed by the sounds of howling women – ageless and primeval. The wooden fan whirred above them but flies already settled near the bed – sickening in their anticipation. Minute winged hyenas. The priest, a family friend, took the liberty of stepping forward with a swat. In hot countries the dead decompose rapidly and are buried within twenty-four hours. Doña Maria rose to her feet, she straightened her dress, dabbed her face and slowly left the room.

'Que calor, que calor,' she murmured to the priest. He smiled in commiseration. Her daughters filed out after her. It was only Luz who turned to look at her father.

'Chau Papa,' she said softly. Her face was pale but serene.

Johnny got up early – six o'clock. Shafts of pale sunshine played on the wallpaper of their room. It shed a radiant light everywhere. Hope. Today could bring results. This time the foreigner seemed more decisive. His enquiries had been lengthy and very detailed. He seemed very sure of what he wanted. They must have spoken for an hour.

Lately Johnny had forgotten prayer. Church for him, though regularly attended had become an almost mechanical thing. When he read the lesson, the lectern seemed a million miles away. Like much else, he had become expert at the motions of life and normality while underneath was a man paralysed with fear. If he could get this deal! If he could get the advance, the company would be saved, his men safe. He and Anna …Well. As he shaved he closed his eyes tight for one brief moment and whispered 'please'. A pink shirt, a blue tie, dark grey trousers and a blazer. Immaculate and handsome – who ever would have guessed that this was a frightened man? He was the picture of calm affluence. Johnny kissed his sleeping wife and went downstairs. Sixpence, the cat, rose languidly and arched when she saw him. Fudge, the chocolate Labrador, wagged his tail. Something wonderfully reassuring about their consistency – and their complete unawareness of the present situation. Johnny stroked them both in turn and then opened the doors. He breathed in the fresh spring air. The world gleamed, the birds sung and everywhere spoke of new growth. Hope. Fudge licked his hand then broke away. He trotted to his habitual spot in the orchard and lifted his leg. Johnny watched him and noted that he was overweight. He could not remember when he had last walked him. It was still very early so he stepped into the garden and joined the new day. Anna's hand was everywhere. The weeding, the pruning, the attempts to tie things back and to stake small trees against the southern winds. She mowed the lawn twice a week starting at the beginning of march. She'd bet herself that she'd hear the cuckoo exactly thirty days later. The newly painted windows on the house had been done by her. Johnny examined them closely. What was he thinking? Where on earth was his energy? His life force? His authority? Had he become a mothered spineless man? Sexless too. He strode towards the old pear tree – just then covered in beautiful white blossom. He put his forehead against the bark. 'Please,' he whispered. The fragrant air caressed his face – but did not hear his plea. The familiar ache of fear, blissfully absent for a few moments now returned to his stomach. He could not bear much more of this.

'Eggs ready!' Jolted his despair. And there she stood by the kitchen door. 'What a day!' Johnny walked towards her. He smiled and she opened her arms to him. A little later she stood at the front door still in her white cotton nightdress and red Wellington boots. She waved until his car disappeared. And as he turned in to the courtyard of his office, he said one last, 'please'.

Yvonne had arrived a little before him. Ritualistically, she plugged in the kettle and got out two mugs for tea. Always cheerful, she kept the office in pristine order and she guarded Johnny like a bulldog. During these last months, she always made sure the good news came first.

'Big day, Mr Carr! Mr.Perez LaCosta at 10 o'clock – fingers crossed.' She gave him a beaming smile. 'You look well today.' She ran her eyes over his clothes and always approved when he wore a tie. He walked in front of her to his room and she followed like a bridesmaid – with his tea.

'No interesting mail today.' She did not want him opening bills that simply could not be paid – or letters of threat.

'I can deal with these while you get yourself ready.' As she turned to leave she said,

'He will be speaking English won't he? It's my only language.' Yvonne looked perplexed. Johnny laughed,

'Swahili, I think.' He said.

'Swa…what?'

'Actually, Yvonne, if we are to be serious about this I think our Mr. LaCosta is either Chilean or from Argentina. In which case Spanish is his language.' Frankly, who cared what he spoke as long as his money was good – and plentiful.

'Don't worry about the way he speaks, Yvonne. Let's just hope his cheque book will do the talking.' Johnny smiled at her again.

'I'll let you get on,' she said, still a little uneasy. She made a mental note to buy an atlas. Where on earth was Chile? Foreigners, all of them, were an enigma to her. The furthest she had ever been was the Isle of Wight for the day – and the relief of getting home was something she never forgot. What colour would he be?

A while later, she rang through.

'He's arrived. I can't see him because the windows of the car are smoked.'

'Thank you, Yvonne. Take his coat when he comes in and just bring him along.'

She nodded to the telephone then said, 'Good luck, Mr. Carr.' Johnny moved things about his desk contriving to make it look busy. Quickly, he opened a drawer and threw a file out. He found several photographs of cars he had restored – famous cars. The Ferrari, a Bugatti, the Fraser Nash. He searched for the Maserati but was interrupted…Yvonne again.

'Oh Mr. Carr – Mr. La Costa has not been able to come.' Johnny slumped.

'His wife has come instead.' He groaned. Oh God, women and cars! Like men and patchwork quilts. He braced himself.

'Show her down, will you.'

'I think she's already with you, Mr. Carr.' Johnny looked up and saw long red nails curled round the side of the door.

'Hello.'

He jumped to his feet. Black hair, black eyes, magnolia skin, wide red mouth. Blazing before him. A perfectly tailored white suit edged with black braiding. Gold buttons, gold bracelets and gold circles swinging from concealed lobes. A shining jewelled watch on a thin wrist. Crocodile shoes supporting perfect legs. Thirty something.

'Good morning to you. I'm Johnny Carr. I'm so glad that you found us – and that you could come.'

'Thank you,' she answered quietly.

'Did you have a good journey – what about some coffee?'

An elegant smile.

'Two questions, all at once! Yes, I had a good journey, thank you – and yes, I'd love some coffee, thank you. But can it please be filtered? Instant coffee does not agree with me.'

Soft voice. Another lovely smile.

'Of course. Do sit down.' She did. Johnny watched her cross her legs. He watched beautiful hands, red-nailed, take out a folder and a gold pen. She placed them tidily before her on his desk and then she surveyed them and satisfied herself that everything was in order. She hid her nerves well.

'Yvonne – two coffees please – filtered.' Via the intercom.

'We only have instant. We've never kept the other stuff. Is she Columbian or something?'

'Thank you, Yvonne – that will be all for now,' he said smoothly and he smiled at Mrs. La Costa.

'Your coffee will be here in a moment,' he told her.

'Now – when did you both arrive in London?'

'Oh, let me think – four days ago only. It seems longer – we have been so busy. I must tell you the reason I am here is because my husband has not been very well.' She shrugged slightly. 'I hope that is all right – that you don't mind. I know this is really a man's world but I know my stuff – oh, is that the right word? Stuff?' Johnny laughed.

He liked her – so straightforward and nice. She continued,

'After all, one of the cars is for me. Did my husband tell you that?' Her face was lit with excitement. She had longed for a car like this.

'Do you mind if I smoke?'

Johnny abhorred smoking, particularly in women. 'Not at all. Please do – I'll find you an ash-tray.' With alacrity he reached the door, shot down the passage and came back with one. 'Here you are,' he said. 'Not very elegant I'm afraid.'

'Who cares?' She waved her hand.

'Have you got a lighter, Mrs. La Costa?'

'Of course I do! Please call me Sol – it is so much shorter. My name is a mouthful – especially at this hour of the morning. It makes a lot of people spit – they can't help it.' Her dark eyes were full of amusement. She studied Johnny carefully from them and was clever the way she engaged him with her easy manner. With her invisible antennae she assessed him and she liked what she saw. She inhaled deeply from her cigarette and she relaxed visibly as she pulled the smoke into her mouth. Then she savoured it.

'I needed this,' she said, holding it up before them. 'You don't?'

'No. No, I don't smoke. Never have.' He didn't add 'filthy habit' as he usually did – because just then he did not feel it was.

'Congratulations. You don't suffer, like I do, from nerves. Your business must be going well.'

'We can't complain. Now...' Johnny wanted to get on with the business. The formalities were now out of the way. He decided to treat her like a man – he'd be very straightforward. He'd make no concessions.

'Now.' He began again. 'What exactly can we do for you – or help you with? Your husband mentioned an interest in Ferraris?' He sounded intentionally vague. She laughed.

'An interest? A passion, you mean! I don't think I can name any other thing on this earth that pleases my husband more than the sight, sound and smell of a Ferrari.' Sol paused – then gave a little shrug. 'I mean it's like a man in love.'

Oh God. Lyrical comparisons jarred with Johnny. His mind was practical and unimaginative – he had a no nonsense approach to his business.

'And for you?' he asked. 'What do you feel about them?' She thought carefully.

'Freedom, freedom, freedom with a capital F. The best I've ever known. Control too I suppose – and power. Are they the same, control and power? Perhaps. I don't know. Anyway,' she waved her hand and dismissed the question. 'I think speed is wonderful. I mean, tell me, what could possibly be better than a long straight road that stretches ahead with no end, the sun, and just yourself sitting in this beautiful thing – whoosh. Off you go!' She brought her eyes back to him.

'A big thrill – like a bunch of tropical flowers delivered after midnight! That's what I feel about Ferraris.' Johnny saw that her face glowed with excitement. There was a freshly innocent enthusiasm that reminded him of his daughter. He had seen the same look on her face. A schoolgirl out for the day.

Sol was thinking too. With her head on one side, she looked at Johnny. She decided that she'd like to make him laugh. So serious, so polite – so correct. She would like to un-British him for at least five minutes – take away that burden-on-the-shoulder demeanour. What a challenge that would be!

'I used to drive one myself. They are beautiful cars, I must agree with you.' So unenthusiastic, so passionless. Sol sat up. Suddenly business-like, she gave a little cough and cleared her throat.

'Well, we want two please.' she requested formally. '1963 or thereabouts. Original chassis –new bodies done here hopefully.' She carefully read her notes, then she pulled out all the papers and handed them to Johnny.

'You will see that Fernando has put everything down here for you. The specifications. Better if you read it all for yourself.'

Yvonne came in then – a little late having had to send out for the coffee. She eyed Sol as a walker might eye a bull in a small field. Never in all her life had she seen such glamour! Or smelt such scent – lilies of the valley! Was she real?

'Thank you so much.' Sol looked at her and gave her a dazzling smile.

'Do you think it possible to bring me some mineral water as well?' Yvonne looked immediately at Johnny.

'Of course we can do that. Yvonne will bring it to you straight away.' Without looking up, inwardly, he trembled with excitement. Suddenly the sun had bounced up on the horizon – the heat, so long in coming, now licked his forehead. It felt good. Sublime. Two Ferraris – not just one. He now needed to formalise the whole project with a fat deposit then he and the company would have reached the shore. Sol cut in to his racing thoughts.

'I must say your Yvonne is quite a character, isn't she? How long has she worked for you?'

'Oh let me think – all of fifteen years I think. Yes. Yes, you are right, she is a character.' He laughed aware that the tightness usually lodged in his throat had gone.

'She reminds me of your English bulldog. You know that dog with that angry look.'

Sol levelled her head and knitted her brow. She lowered the corners of her mouth and jutted out her lower lip. Her impression was brilliant. Johnny threw back his head and laughed so loudly that the men could hear him in the workshop.

'Boss sounds happy,' said one.

'Must be good news.'

'Bloody hope so – save our bacon.'

'She thinks I'm some sort of monster I think – or just a bloody foreigner.' Quickly, Sol put her hand over her mouth.

'Oh my goodness, forgive me. I didn't mean to use that horrid word. But you know what I mean.' She smiled ruefully. 'I just know that the English are not mad about people from other lands, are they? It's just our money they like.' She thought a little – becoming serious.

'Sad, isn't it? Money is a language all on its own. Anyway, where were we? Oh yes – how long will all this take do you think? Gestation varies so much doesn't it?'

Another cigarette now took up all her attention. She performed the whole act of lighting up so elegantly – her accessories matching her perfectly – the gold cigarette case, her matching lighter. Her fine hands tipped with crimson, her red mouth – both conspirators in the art of nicotine worship. Her absorption in what she did fascinated Johnny and it was only after a long inhalation that she returned to the office and to him. She realised he watched her.

'My husband says you are the best. Is it true?'
Johnny shrugged. 'At least we survived the recession. That says something, I suppose.'

'Well we always read about you – and the things you have done.'

'Well, that's good,' he said. 'It's a funny old business this. One moment you are up and overloaded with work – the next it can all change. It is perhaps the most precarious of all art forms.'

Sol frowned slightly.

'Yes. I suppose it is art – I had not thought of it that way before. And you have survived the commercial side – as you say, others have not.' Johnny changed the subject.

'What car do you drive?'

'At the moment a Mercedes Sports. But I battle with Luca, my son, every day as he is always taking it from me.'

'Really? Is he old enough to drive?'

'Luca? Of course! I was married when I was sixteen you see.'

'Good Lord!' Johnny was genuinely shocked. 'Is that normal?'

'Don't I look normal?' She suddenly jumped to her feet and did a little twirl for him. Lithe, supple and strong. She laughed with unaffected fun at her show of physical proof.

'Well, what do you think? Do I pass the test?' She sat down and explained.

'Fernando is much older than me – I suppose we had to hurry up! Anyway, if you are born in a hot country and sun-fed like I was, you grow up quickly. Reaching for the light you see. Just like a pineapple. You become a woman very young and if you aren't too hideous – someone marries you! I was a child bride I suppose.' She laughed lightly. 'Are you married?'

'Very much so,' he answered punctually. 'For years, in fact – we have three children – all grown up and my wife …'

'I know, I know, don't tell me – she spends all her time in the garden, she wears no make-up and she looks after everyone. Am I right?' Sol leant towards him, her eyes ran over his face – she x-rayed him. 'Hm. I can see that I am.' She was humorously satisfied. She sat back then.

'God – why is it British women simply don't care?'

He had never considered the question so his reply came back rather feebly, with no backbone or conviction,

'Care? Of course they care – in their way.' He wanted it to go no further. Stop. He spread his hands on the table and said,

'Now is there anything else that you need to know today? If I may, I will speak to your husband tomorrow. We will do the preliminary costings today and get those to him by courier. I'd like to meet him – when do you think that might be possible?'

'A little later this week?' She frowned slightly. 'I just hope he does not become unwell again.'

'Is there any reason to think he might?' Johnny tried to mask his horror. 'Surely not.'

'Well, he is seventy-five you see.' She started to gather up her things. Very neatly. Very organised. She put everything away and zipped up the ostrich skin folder. She hugged it against her. A shadow had fallen over her face – it emanated from her eyes. Before he had thought properly, Johnny said,

'Lunch! Let me take you out to lunch.'

She raised her head quickly. It made her black silky hair shudder and gleam. She gave him her most radiant smile.

'Really?' she said. 'Let's. Thank you, Johnny.'

Outside the office door and on the floor, stood two bottles of mineral water. Quite forgotten, they stood like sentry soldiers. Sol scooped one up and unscrewed the top with surprising haste. She drank from it like some greedy sailor. Johnny hid his amusement. This was business.

Ten miles away, Anna struggled hard to concentrate on her flower- bed. She weeded with speed and a disciplined thoroughness that failed just then to assuage her energy. She needed something much more demanding. She grabbed a spade and marched to the rose bed. Every bit of her screamed to be absorbed. She plunged it into the dark, silent soil. Her movements could have been mistaken for anger or abnormal behaviour, so exuberant was her digging. She wasn't angry – just so worried she could not sit still. Today of all days! Hope had given way to a sort of buckling hopelessness. So near. Was the fight nearly over? Could this be the day that turned things round? Such endurance! Another disappointment and Johnny would collapse. She was certain of it. It made her panicky. She was dead tired. Exhausted. The tears came. Large swollen drops that felt the size of grapes They slid down her face splashing on her spade, the earth. Her small shoulders shuddered and in a gesture of angry despair, she threw the spade from her like some ancient harpoon. Her strength surprised her – when she saw where it lay.

'How much more of this?' she asked a silent sky. Its confident dazzling perfection offered her no reply. Wretched.

'What a fool.' Straightening herself up she took in a deep breath. 'Come on, Fudge. Let's go.'
She marched to the fence, swung over and took the track that led to the hill. Her dog trotted beside her already panting at the speed they went.

'Come on,' she said again. 'Let's walk all day if that's what it takes. There is nothing else to do – and it's free.' She looked down at the shiny brown head.

'It's free, Fudge – do you understand?' And suddenly she wanted to laugh hysterically, like some toothless old hag. Insane. It was terrifying to be so out of control.

Up, up the hill they went and over the top to the other side – breath-taking in panoramic beauty, but she hardly looked up. Nor did she notice a jogger running past. He saw her though but decided to say nothing on seeing her face. Instead, he spurted on. It was only when he got home that he thought perhaps he should have said something to her. Poor woman. Obviously very upset about something.

Natural beauty pacifies and provides natural balm. Anna felt it, and it wasn't long before she felt bathed in a merciful calm. It seeped through her. Out here and above it all, nothing could touch her. A heavenly haven from earthly troubles. She regained control as she had done a thousand times before. Defiant now, she threw fear out of her stomach. It allowed her to crumple and fall like a rag doll on the grass. Fudge did the same. Anna lay quite still on her back and she gazed at the infinite blue sky. A long time ago, when she was young, she had done this beneath a bluer and more vibrant sky. It somehow did the trick for her – so pure, so inaccessible and yet so intimately entwined to every living thing.

Her mind drifted and found peace in travelling back to those times. The sky then had enabled her to do good – would it today be her mascot again? Absurd! She smiled sleepily at such a thought. Life was not a fairy tale any more – as it had been then.

She reached out her arm and touched Fudge.

'Crisis over,' she murmured. He had been watching her all the time, alert to her mood. He knew she was unhappy. He moved towards her and licked her hand. She lent on her elbow and put her forehead against his. He gazed at her from mournful, watchful eyes.

Much later, beyond afternoon, she made her way down. She detoured a little and went into the little church that stood in the middle of a field. With two hands she turned the cumbersome old door handle. She went in and sat down on the hard, austere pew. A cold silence enveloped her. Light filtered through the windows on the west side – beautiful, pale, holy. If God was here, why was he sometimes not outside? Invisible, absent. Unhearing. Where did he go in the small hours of night? Did he ever catch her words then? Anna shut her eyes but did not kneel. She was alone. God did not expect her to kneel. She said out loud, 'Help us. Please help us.' Her words hung like swollen bubbles – suspended in the air – then silence caught their fall. Nothing came back to her. Instinctively, she knew she had to be patient. There were more seven-bar gates to jump. She opened her eyes, looked up and levelled them at the cross.

It stood some way from her pew but she saw it plainly.

No suffering on earth could ever be as lonely and painful as that. A mother's suffering parallel in mental depth – her heart broken by a son now out of reach, her mind bewildered by a sense of betrayal and the physical proof of despair. Mother and son shattered apart by torture – then death. A lump rose in Anna's throat – her situation could never match this. It would be disgraceful to think otherwise.

She jumped at the sound of Fudge barking. It ripped through her thoughts.

'Thought the red boots were yours.'

She spun round. Robin, the young vicar, stood in the aisle not far off. He laughed. His silent entry disconcerted her. She hoped he had not been there too long.

'I've come to collect a book.'

As he approached, he saw her discomfort – the tired eyes. Anna got to her feet. She was embarrassed.

'Hello, Robin,' she smiled at him. It quite transformed her face – took the edges of sadness away. 'I'm just going.' She walked quickly passed him. 'Bye,' she called. The door slammed behind her. The noise resounded around the church and made the bats in the roof dart out briefly.

'God bless.' He replied. He looked towards the altar and said, 'Help her, Lord, in her distress.' He stood a full minute in reverence, then bowed and turned to the vestry door.

·· ·· ·· ·· ··

'Goodness you look tired, darling!'

'And you stink of wine!' She was so pleased to see him again. She hugged him to her and put her head on his chest.

'I haven't seen you for ages – at least it seems like that.' Her day, a Himalayan ordeal now over, normality regained. Johnny was back. He looked different. He looked wonderful! A healthy colour suffused his face and his eyes sparkled.

'Well?' She broke away from him. 'Well?'

'Don't go.' He pulled her back. His voice thicker, more languid. With lips against her hair, he said,

'We're there, I think!' Tremulous voice. 'Two Ferraris, no less.'

Anna squeezed him, her arms belt-like around his waist. She shut her eyes and listened to the steady thudding of his heart. She felt her fears slip away.

'This evening I must finish off the work – get all the costings ready to be sent tomorrow morning. The deposit alone will be enough to save us all, do you realise that, Anna?' She stood on tiptoe and kissed him, utterly at one with his joy.

'We will be safe? The house won't have to go?' A shared silence enveloped them.

'Oh Johnny,' she murmured.

'Was he nice – a nice foreigner?'

'Very,' he replied. 'Charming in fact – from Argentina. Very rich. Frankly that's all that matters.' He gave a short laugh.

'Married?'

'Yes. Married. One son and …'

'Drenched in beastly cologne. You stink of lilies of the valley – ugh!' Anna got closer to her husband.

'Did he wear those two-toned shoes?'

Johnny laughed again. 'Really, Anna, what a question. I don't go round looking at people's feet you know!'

'Well they all do,' she told him playfully.

'Perhaps,' he stroked her hair methodically. 'A long time ago perhaps – but not now.'

She continued to tease him. 'Handbag?'

Johnny put her at arm's length. 'Anna this is quite enough! You are talking about our saviour. I'm now going to shut myself in the study and I shan't come out until I've finished the figures.' He patted her bottom.

'And I will bring you a drink,' she told him sweetly.

Johnny closed the study door. Immediately he asked himself, 'Have I lied to her?' Why? Not exactly. Not directly. More an evasion of precise detail. Nothing more than that. But in all the years of their married life, he had never resorted to this sort of deception. He had never been economical with the truth – he had never had to be.

'Well, Chiquita – how did it all go. I want to hear everything.' Fernando embraced his wife and then kissed her smooth forehead. 'A drink?'

She smiled at her husband and nodded.

'Hm. Please. A bucket of mineral water would be nice. I have had such a good day, Fernando.' Her red lips, freshly painted for him, parted in a huge and radiant smile. 'Mr. Carr is a lovely man. Very British – so correct! Fernando, it would make you laugh so much. But he is charming too and clever. You should see all the cars they have down there!' Sol busied herself with her gloves. Her eyes concentrated on removing them while she spoke – her teeth tugged at the ungiving leather fingers.

'He will have everything ready for you by tomorrow. I left him all your papers – that was the right thing to do, wasn't it?' She pouted her mouth and frowned slightly.

'It was such a pity you could not come, Fernando.' She left her gloves on the sofa and walked over to him. She took her husband's hand and held it against her waist. With the other hand, she touched his face. She responded to the devotion she saw coming from his eyes.

'I've missed you,' he said.

'Yes – I know – but now you are feeling better, Querido. A day on your own has done you good, hasn't it?' Her eyes studied him carefully. 'You look much better,' she told him softly. And then,

'Will we be dining out?' she asked. He basked in her concern for him. He had schooled her well in the care of her man. Her hands, like a pair of creamy doves, now flitted about his face. They soothed him. Air travel these days exhausted him but he did not want to disappoint her.

'Where would you like to go, my angel?'

'Oh, I don't know. Perhaps we should just slip downstairs tonight, wouldn't that be better? The food is fine.' She smiled at him – attentively. He noted her softness – her gentle calm.

'But have you eaten properly today, Chiquita?' he asked with velvet tenderness.

'Just a sandwich in the car – I didn't feel like anything more.'

She walked away from him then and went to the bathroom. She shut the door. Click. She looked at herself in the brilliantly lit mirror. It reflected her lovely day.

'I've lied to him.' she said, in a low voice. She gulped and felt a little flicker of panic. 'I've lied to him about the sandwich.' Was that all? Surely that wasn't so bad. She moved about, turned on the taps so that they gushed and swilled away her guilt. She freshened her face – composed herself – her little secret of happiness. She returned to her husband, put her arms around his neck and kissed his cheek.

'I'm sorry I have been away all day,' she said.

.. ..

'Darling! Come and eat.'

> '*In Argentina we eat steaks like this.*' Red tipped nails – pale olive hands measuring a generous inch between thumb and forefinger. '*They are called bifes.*'

Johnny sat down at the square kitchen table. A perfect dinner was set out before him. Anna had rushed out to pick some old-fashioned roses and put them in the small silver bowl. She had made him his favourite fish pie.

> 'We eat late at night – all the year round.'

Anna handed Johnny his plate. She caught his eyes with her own and smiled.

> 'The summers are long and of course, very hot. We leave for our estancia generally in November. I ride a lot early in the morning to catch the best part of the day – the best air. I love best of all to see the sun come over the lagoon. The flamingos. It always excites me – a new day.   At that hour the whole world seems to be full of anticipation . Do you understand what I mean by that? It's a sort of optimism, I suppose. Do you feel the same?'

Sixpence smelt the fish and came near enough to weave herself around their legs. Anna beamed at Johnny. She felt truly happy tonight.

'Here's to us, darling.' She raised her glass of wine to him. He did the same. They smiled at each other and then drank.

> 'The best wines – red – are grown in Mendoza. That's a province in the mid-north-west. A beautiful area of wonderful valleys and sheltering hills. It would be nice to   buy a vineyard one day. We drink so much wine – little children do as well – it is part of the culture, part of their   upbringing. Diluted with soda, of course. You'd love it   there, Johnny.'

'Hm. This pie is delicious, Anna. You always do it so well – more please.' He pushed his plate towards her.

'I thought we might deserve a treat tonight, so I added salmon and prawns.' He watched her spoon a second helping.

'And what did you get up to today? Were you in the garden – I bet you were?'

'Don't tell me – let's see – she likes gardening.'

'Not exactly. I started off there but I couldn't stay in it for long. I walked instead.'

'Where did you go?'

'Oh, up the hill via Carter's meadow. Fudge and I tramped all day – didn't we?' Anna stroked his faithful head that rested heavily on her thigh.

'Then we took the same track the horses take. It was so lovely on the top – like being half way up to the sky. I wish you could have been with us.'

She would not tell him how hellish her day had been. How she had worried about him. Her little visit to the church. Robin. He would say nothing. Anyway, it now seemed irrelevant and nothing to do with the present.

'Did you really marry at sixteen?'

'I did. I met my husband in November and we were married in March. Can you imagine? I didn't have time to think – or breathe! Well at that age girls don't think, they just do what they are told. Perhaps their bodies do the thinking. I don't know. Can't

remember. He was so kind, so attentive. He picked me out from all my friends – and that made me feel so important. I imagined he was like some god whose hand had touched my shoulder. Ridiculous isn't it to be so romantic? He taught me everything; how to dress, about art, theatre, travel – you know – all the things you teach your own child. He adored me! We had our little son and then of course... What do you think happened next? He did what they all do – he got a mistress! No, don't look shocked, it's quite normal over there. And do you know something? I really didn't mind. I was too absorbed, too in love with my little boy. Besides, he continued to worship me.'

'Are you listening, Johnny – you aren't listening. What are you thinking about?'
'I am listening, darling – it's just that half my head is full of today and all the things I must get done before tomorrow.'

'In our culture, girls are not expected to do much – but oh how I would love to have studied.'
'What in particular?'
'Art and art history. I paint you know – quite well actually.'
Laughter cascaded all over the table, causing heads to turn in surprised curiosity.
'Do you exhibit?'
'I do. And I sell quite a few.'

> *'I can imagine that they are full of colour.'*
> *'Some are, some aren't. Too much colour can take the subtlety out of a picture but of course colour gives joie, doesn't it? And naiveté, oddly enough. But it depends, you know – moods affect the way I paint.'*

'Johnny! For God's sake listen to me. Do you want ice-cream? The home-made stuff?'

'Hm. Please. Love some, darling. Then I must finish off my work. It won't take too long.' He caught her hand as she passed. 'This is a lovely supper – thank you.' He kissed her wrist.

> *'I often paint late at night. You can see so much in the dark. Your imagination can fly up and join the stars – become part of the cosmic sphere. It is something I never tire of. It inspires me to invent amazing things, shapes – like a primitive stage setting on which to put yourself.'* She sighed. *'The world is so beautiful, Johnny – like a wonderful, precious, multi-faceted jewel – don't you think?'*

'Don't be too late, darling. Big day for you tomorrow and you need your sleep. Off you go! I'll do this.' Anna stood in the middle of the kitchen between Johnny and the sink. Very upright and very determined that he should do as she said. He smiled at her, his eyes twinkled.

'My wife has very pink cheeks tonight,' he said. It was true. Anna's face glowed.

'Must be drunk,' she said, touching her face with a fleeting hand. 'Whatever it is, it is a wonderful feeling!' And again, 'Now off you go.'

'See you in a while.'

> *'Does this restaurant offer rooms? I always have a siesta, no matter what or where. People don't here do they? It should be made law. Everyone would be much nicer – better looking too. Can you ask for me please? Thank you, Johnny. You are the kindest man I know.'*

When is adultery, " adultery"? Is it the lustful glance? The first words of blatant flattery, the silent imagination that burns with unspeakable longing? The contemplation of illicit pleasure. Or is it the act itself? The heaving, sweating bodies fused in ludicrous positions like animals snatching at meat – both with an eye on the clock. Because clock there always is. That timely reminder of guilt. Nothing is more stomach punching than that.

Acts such as these committed daily (and nightly) by countless thousands are rarely acts of love. They are frantic stabs of escapism; sensual oblivion of the most flawed kind. But who cares? At the intoxicating time, no one. To hell with it – Carpe Diem. Adultery is available to anyone who seeks it – hey ho. It is easily justified – the common denominator being that there is nothing left at home. What used to be has now been subtly eroded – two angry people now share an uneasy bed, silently screaming in the dark to be elsewhere. Neither admits to it. Furtively, they seek pleasure elsewhere and discover that the night has its own laws.

Victoria, who specialised in divorce, said, 'It is only social convention that has created monogamy in order to maintain a tidy social order, that's all. Basically, I think we are all polygamous.'
Honor, who specialised in housekeeping, said, 'Rubbish! Adultery is dreadful. I'd kill Gerald is he was unfaithful. I never would be.'
Smiley, who specialised in hedonism (and avoiding marriage) said, 'Oh for heaven's sake, live for the moment. Life is to be enjoyed. It's not some continual penance, you know. The French have it all down to a fine art. Good wine and good adultery rules their lives. Everyone knows – nobody cares. It works very well.'
And Anna – what did she say?
 'There's nothing to say. It is a subjective matter. Your conscience says it for you. And if that isn't compass enough, then read the Ten Commandments.'
But, typically, she did not actually reveal her own thoughts on the subject. Gob smacking delivery – but did she allow for human fallibility? The three women said nothing. Instead, Victoria shrugged. Honor nodded in approval. She interpreted what Anna said as an affirmation of her own feelings. Smiley winked, at no one in particular – and then she lit a cigarette.

Fernando read the pages. Every specification was listed and priced. He was impressed with the presentation, the very detailed description of the work in hand and the speed it had been done. The hall-porter had brought it up early on a silver tray. Fernando had tipped the boy and patted his shoulder.

'Thank you, young man.' He was always ready to pay for service, ever courteous no matter to whom. His impeccability matched his dress. Fernando adored England and everything English. He admired its people – their formality – their informality. Their tolerance. He learnt the subtle rules of friendship. Once common ground was established and unspoken trust recognised, friendship with an Englishman was for life. Fernando mastered the groundwork very quickly and he ingratiated himself with elegance. He had many friends here. He understood the rules perfectly and remained always very sensitive to them – at least on the surface. He was something of a chameleon.

Sol lent over his shoulder. She read the estimate. Her black hair tickled the side of his face. He could feel her all about him.

'Well – Mr. Carr seems to know what he is talking about. Most impressive,' he said after a while. His tone indicated satisfaction. He reached and took Sol's hand.

'No wonder you have been so excited, Chiquita. His place must be fascinating – and immaculate too, I imagine.'

Although he could not see her face, he was sure she was smiling. She was! Broadly.

'Well Fernando – what do you think? Will we go ahead?'

'Of course! Do I have a choice?' It was his turn to smile now. He loved to please her.

'Oh, Fernando! Thank you, thank you.' She rushed round to face him and threw her arms around his neck. Like a child, he thought. He adored this side of her – so sweet. Her face was flushed with excitement.

'Very expensive sweets,' he joked. 'But I'm sure they will taste delicious. So now! When do we go down?' Then more to himself,

'I'll ring Mr. Carr now – make the arrangements…'

'Shall I?' she asked breathlessly. And quickly added, 'Would that be a help?'

'No. No, Chiquita.' He got to his feet. 'Certainly not – this is man's stuff.'

And he patted her cheek.

It was good to hear Johnny singing in his bath. Anna lay back on the pillows that she had stacked behind her – and felt happy. Suddenly their world was safe – they could tiptoe away from the vertical plunge that a few days ago had promised to swallow them. They would have tumbled rapidly – down, down into the utterly humiliating mouth of bankruptcy. It would receive them with a diabolical grin on its face. Floundering, they would have clung together searching for metaphorical lifejackets. Johnny would not have survived – she knew that. But now – bliss. Anna curled her legs and pulled the sheets up to her chin. She felt alive. Restored. Attractive.

Yvonne had decided she did not trust Mrs. Perez LaCosta.

'I smell a rat,' she informed her husband. 'You should see her. Sort of woman that gobbles up a man. You know what I mean – he doesn't stand a chance, poor devil!' She frowned.

'Lennie – what's that insect called, you know, the one that eats the male after they've…'

'Praying Mantis.' He smiled kindly at her then said, 'Come on, Yvonne, what's got into you? Never heard you talk like this before – sure you aren't imagining things?'

'Nope.' Her mouth as straight as a rail-track. 'Mr. Carr is on hot coals. You should see him, Lennie. Anyone would think he'd never seen a woman before.' Pause. Dilemma.

'Course, she is native. That sort of woman is different, I can see that. So you can't compare the two women can you? Mrs. Carr is a lovely lady – she cares for everybody. But the other is just plain…'

'Sexy?' Again Lennie supplied the word.

'Hmm, I suppose you could say that. If you like that sort of thing.'

'Most men do, luv.'

'Lennie!' He shrugged his shoulders.

'Put the kettle on, old thing. Let's talk about something else. What others do is their own business – not ours.'
His wife walked over to the tap. He watched with amusement in his blue English eyes. He didn't dare tell her then that she'd put on weight. Not today.

'Anyway, I shan't be getting anymore of that filthy coffee she likes. It just won't be available, Lennie. And that water will be out of stock too. Sorry, Mrs. PL – bring your own!'

Lennie laughed out loud then. It was good to see the wife so exercised. He did feel Mr. Carr could look after himself – if he wanted to. A very nice man.

'Come on, luv, let's take our tea into the garden. I want to see how the runner beans are going on.' He took the tray from her.

'Shan't clean out the ashtray either,' she muttered more to herself as she followed Lennie to the vegetable patch.

Johnny arrived very early to the office. He wanted to make absolutely sure that everything was immaculate. The LaCostas were due at 10.00. He had asked Yvonne to be there early too.

Reluctantly she complied. He wanted to double-check everything including the coffee supply – and the water.

'Will Mrs. Carr be coming in today?' she asked him as she took off her coat and hat.

'Mrs. Carr?' Johnny was astounded. 'Why do you ask?' He laughed at the suggestion while he moved about the office with oat-fed energy. Poe-faced, Yvonne watched him straightening this, moving that, picking up and re-arranging magazines. All quite unnecessary in her opinion. He saw the ashtray, picked it up and cleaned it thoroughly with his own handkerchief. He placed it carefully back on the desk.

'You forgot to do this.' he told her. Yvonne decided to say nothing. If she did, she'd probably say too much. Just then she was not in the best of moods.

'I'll go and make your tea,' she told him shortly. Johnny caught her tone and decided she did not like the early hour.

'Too bad,' he thought.
They arrived punctually at 10.00.

'I hope our British observation of Big Ben impresses you, Mr. Carr.' Fernando got out first.
He shook Johnny's hand with both his own; his warm smile accompanying his words. Johnny looked into clever dark eyes and a smile that was both automatic and charming.

'We are both so excited, you see.' He turned to look for his wife. She came and stood by him, silent as a shadow. He put his arm around her shoulders. He laughed and said,

'There is no one more excited that this one!' He looked at her playfully.

'Good morning to you both.' Johnny was nervous, Sol subdued. He smiled formally at the couple and studiedly averted his eyes from the blazing terrible beauty that was her.

'This way.' Johnny held out an arm indicating the way to his office. They followed.
Here, Fernando stopped to shake Yvonne's hand. He asked her how she was? Did she enjoy her work? Where did she live? Was that her car outside – the yellow one? He listened carefully to all her replies. She was dazzled by him – his

courtesy! No one had ever spoken to her like that before. For five brief minutes, she was centre-stage – a film star! And his English – well, who could fault it?

She bolted to the little store cupboard and standing on a chair, she reached to the back of it and fished out the real coffee.

'A lovely man,' she said to herself. 'He deserves this.'

The meeting got underway quickly and went just as Johnny had hoped. Everything dovetailed in according to how he had hoped it might. There appeared to be no modifications. The entire project, time schedule and costing were agreed on both sides. They coincided in everything. Uncannily easy – no sweat. Fernando sat back satisfied. He told Johnny that the deposit money would be with him tomorrow. Suddenly, with one signature, there would be no more problems. Gone! They wanted two cars – they had the money. They'd pay as and when stipulated. Perversely, Johnny could not believe it was happening. This was the oasis he'd been walking towards for months. The water from this well now saved his life. Would one signature really put everything right? It seemed absurdly easy. But yes! was the answer. Yes!

Sol, meanwhile, remained silent. She watched the two men and listened carefully to everything that was being said. Her expression was remarkably serious – and she did not show any signs of joy. She frowned when some of the details were beyond her understanding but she refrained from asking any questions. Occasionally, she'd nod. She was very much an onlooker. Fernando chuckled all morning – he loved negotiations – they had been his life. He particularly relished working with the English. Their whole approach was quite different – so thorough, so meticulous to detail. Naïve too – in a way that amused him. Or perhaps it was their sense of integrity that he did not entirely share or agree with. Or understand. He had learnt that in business that sort of work ethic did not get you very far. Life had taught him to be street-wise – see an advantage and take it. Ruthless like a shark. Yes, business in England amused him. This was the land of trust – of being taken at your word.

They took two hours to finalise things and once completed, Johnny took them to the workshop.
In there, Fernando talked to each man giving him his entire attention. Ambassadorial in manner, he fixed his clever brown eyes on them. He praised everything – and everyone – finishing with comradely slaps on the shoulder. There were smiles on every face by the time he had finished.

From there, Johnny took them to lunch. The air of celebration continued – the food was good and the conversation easy. The two men found they had quite a lot to say to one another. The LaCostas appreciated his attention, the restaurant, and the day. Johnny was affable and socially very professional. The hidden core of him burst with relief.

It was not until the brandy arrived that he was suddenly aware that Fernando's eyes pierced him over the rim of his glass. He was being watched. Like two dark daggers – they sent him a silent but palpable warning. Uncomfortable and unnerved, Johnny looked away. An icy hand seemed to settle on his chest. Sol remained fairly quiet, apparently unaware of the momentary disquiet. She was outwardly serene – and as enigmatic as a Madonna. At the end of lunch, she searched nervously for her cigarettes. Her hands moved anxiously about her bag.

'You are quiet today, my darling.' Fernando said this at various times. He always accompanied the remark with a small laugh and a kiss. Johnny did not attempt to light her cigarette. Lunch ended on a relaxed note – the momentary discord apparently vanished.

It was not until they were on the motorway heading for London that Fernando relaxed his façade. He was not a fool. He had of course noted the studied avoidance that his wife and Mr. Carr shared in not looking at each other – scarcely once in fact. Their sin was obvious. Immediately he felt a little shudder of anger in his stomach. He said nothing. Carefully, he turned to look at his wife. She slept. It allowed him all the time in the world to study that perfect face which generally gave him such pleasure. His virgin wife! Could it be possible? Was he simply imagining things? Fernando would not tolerate infidelity in a wife. He would not be made a fool of – by anyone. Least of all, an Englishman. She was not to be shared. This did not mean he had to be a faithful husband. Men were different.

He had never not had a mistress throughout his life with Sol. But women – they had to obey their husbands. He would teach her a lesson she'd never forget. Sol moved her head then but did not wake. They had reached Knightsbridge before her eyes opened again.

'It would have been so nice to stay longer in the country, wouldn't it?' she said.

'We have the embassy tonight, querida – you must look your best.'

Anna's father had died when she was twelve. His death, so sudden and therefore the more shocking was the worst thing that Anna could ever have imagined. With him went everything that made her days. From laughter to knowledge he had been her guide, teacher – her compass. She froze. And her mother froze with her. They became locked in ice, petrified. The period that followed became the basis that made Anna the person she was to be. A springboard from which to raise her arms above her head, stand taut on tiptoe and then jump into life. She thawed with the natural resilience of the young – she re-found the light and it was brighter than before her father's death. Her mother did not. She retreated from the world and decided not to recover. Anna looked after her like an angel – she was certain that her father watched all the time. She could feel him all about her. She saw him too. His arms crossed against his chest, a half-smile on his dear face. She asked her mother if she ever saw him – her mother replied,

'Of course not, Anna – your father is dead.' And that was the end of the subject.

When she was fourteen she went to boarding school and to her utter amazement she had a wonderful time. It was only then that she realised what a burden her mother was to her. She felt guilty and told no one. Home now gave her clipped wings. School the very opposite – a freedom she had never known. She excelled, made millions of friends and before she knew it – she was eighteen.

Her godfather told her she should now travel, see the world and meet people. Far more useful than a secretarial course. She agreed. She would go anywhere, she told him – with his help and approval. Very quickly, he organised for her to go to Argentina, live with a family and speak English to the three daughters. Without giving it a second thought, she boarded a boat and sailed across the Atlantic to Buenos Aires.

Anna was tremulous with excitement as the boat moved slowly up the muddy River Plate. It was early but the day already promised heat. She lent against the railings and in the distance she could see Panama hats and men in white suits on the quay. She saw waving handkerchiefs too and heard shouts of welcome. Somewhere music played. And once alongside she looked down on shiny heads, bright silk dresses and a thing she never forgot – everyone was smiling.

The family identified her at once. She stood before five impeccably dressed people who all in turn came forward and kissed her. The father spoke first.

'I am Juan Martinez\Acevedo and this is my family.' He swept his hat off his head and she looked into eyes that danced with fun and kindness.

'This is my wife, Maria and these are my girls – Isabel, Maria Marta and my baby, Luz.' He clapped his hands.

'Papa – I am fourteen – I am not your baby.'

'Oh – but you are!' And he laughed. They all did.

'We are all here to welcome Miss Anna Forrester who is our guest and has come all the way from England. You have come to civilise our girls, have you not?' He turned his smiling eyes on her and the rest of the family did the same.

'I will do my best.' Anna heard herself saying seriously – and the three girls dissolved into fits of giggles. He replaced his hat, called the chauffeur and told him to deal with the luggage. His wife had so far not said much, but she smiled a great deal and Anna could see she was kind and reserved. Religious too – she wore a crucifix prominently against a beautiful and expensive dress.

Maria Acevedo had been brought up exclusively to make a good marriage – and stick to it. She did not disappoint. Her husband had been the catch of the day – and she the obvious choice. Their families had from the start cast them together as a pair. It made perfect sense. Money, land and breeding should always marry – money, land and breeding! So when she walked up the aisle aged eighteen she had every right to smile serenely. She was pleasing everyone. Her twenty-four year old groom was thrilled with her – they were bound by the catholic sense of doing what was right. Their marriage had been a lavish affair. A 10.00 pm ceremony in a sombrely lit church and then a reception for no less than two thousand people in Buenos Aires' smartest club. They danced until sunrise and were lovers by 9.00 am. And exactly nine months later Isabel was born. Society nodded its approval. Maria's life became, at the tender age of nineteen, dutiful, submissive – safe and happy. She adored her husband and it pleased her totally to obey him in everything. She was not particularly beautiful then but as she grew older she became very striking – she learnt how to beguile. Throughout her life, her face retained an innocence that belongs only to women who do not take lovers and who dedicate themselves to the love of one man. Hers was a face you could not ignore. Her husband could not be ignored either. Demonstrative, effusive and always appeared to be in a good mood. He was lucky – unlatin in that he was neither moody nor overly volatile. Nor was he dark and swarthy. Nor typically handsome. His face was open, merry and a good healthy colour. He was tall for a latin and very athletic. He rode a great deal; was skilled on the polo field and loved his chestnut mares. He had fine sensitive hands – they told you of strength and kindness. And when he spoke (which he did often) they accompanied his every word, backing up his views, reinforcing his opinions. People loved him and wanted his approval. When Anna arrived, he was forty-four, his wife four years younger. They were in the prime of their lives – besotted with their three girls. Theirs was a privileged life, understatedly glamorous. They were asked everywhere and seen everywhere. They conducted themselves modestly and were noted for their generosity and united marriage. They had a vast house in the capital, set off a tree-lined street and four farms in various parts of the land. Juan Acevedo administered them himself; not to do so, he said, was asking for trouble. He flew from farm to farm piloting himself in his Cessna plane. He planned his weeks to return home at the weekends to his waiting women. He filled the house with light – even the staff in the kitchen smiled to one another on hearing his voice. He chased his daughters all over the house, teasing them relentlessly – always the same theme. Whichever one he caught, he'd command her to marry a good man – forbid her an ugly one. He wanted only beautiful grandchildren to fill up every corner of the house and 'so does your mama.' The rooms reverberated with high-pitched shrieks and running footsteps. He chased Anna too, when he got to know her better and saw that she was no longer shy of him. He told her she'd not be allowed to leave, ever; and that he would personally select a husband for her – a good man, a rich man – how about that? That way she would be with them forever. Ha! Now wasn't that a good plan? Juan was thrilled with the idea and highly amused with his little plan. Anna had no idea that families behaved like this and she loved every minute of it. His wife watched on. She was unfailingly humoured by him and his ridiculous games. She often clapped her hands together and bent her head in laughter. She smiled at him the same way a mother smiles at her beloved son – indulgently – allowing him all the freedoms he wanted. Her smiles used to be flirtatious – they used to invite him to her bed.

Summer came. The city became stunningly hot, suffocating at midday. Ice-cream vendors stood everywhere on street corners – beneath trees that showed off their lovely Jacaranda flowers. By day the city was subdued – waiting. It waited for dark to bring out walking lovers, families, groups of elderly ladies, beautifully dressed – all relieved the day was over. The restaurants filled, people sat in doorways, watched from balconies – in a huge shared sigh of pleasure. Life at night after a day of heat is sensuous – silky. Quite separate from day.

The family packed up the house and left for one of the farms. They took their staff with them. It was near the coast – a vast, rambling house, surrounded by oaks, ancient magnolias, and fir trees of all description. And beyond the park, acres of flat endless land. Anna's English eyes, quite inexperienced to such magnitude, took time to adjust. To her, it seemed the land flew away from beneath her sandalled feet racing until it hit the line of blue sky on a horizon that could be a million miles away. Like a vast arch, the sky crowned and dominated everything. More sky than land! Now that was new optic illusion – and the effect very powerful. At first, Anna was quietly unnerved by this phenomenon – aware too of an outrageous sense of freedom. Here was geography unharnessed and untamed. Eucalyptus grew all over the land in long lines for barriers against the winds, in groups for shade. They were the principal feature and broke up the monotony that threatened to distract the eye. Windmills stood in every field like proud all-weather flowers, they punctuated the flatness; announced animal presence – human too. A relief. It was with awe that Anna studied the land. She met it on her terms – it would not overpower her. Gradually, she allowed herself to succumb to its raw titillating beauty.

She grew to love the vast open space that was inescapably all around her.

She found her paints, her easel – she could not stop. Beneath this vibrant almost virgin beauty, she saw blues and yellows properly for the first time. A field of sunflowers before they were heavy with seed was a sight that stopped her heart. A yellow so perfect, so strong – its colour unchanged beneath the moon. She painted them as they grew and became powerful in their prime. And then they hung their heads, like children in shame. She painted their humiliation, full of ripe dark seeds. A representation – a metaphorical illusion on birth, life, death. The results thrilled her, the experience unexpectedly emotional – oddly fulfilling. From then on the vast herds of cattle, the men on their horse, their incredible skill, their puestos (houses), all entered her drawing book . She loved to watch as women washed their children beneath water pumps; their laughter always present. Strong white teeth, thick black hair. She could live like this forever – why not? She dreamt of becoming a famous artist.

Anna shared a room with Luz. High ceiling, white walls and a large wooden fan above them could not keep the heat out that night. The two girls lay wide awake – restless. It was well past midnight. The house was silent. The night humid and still, not a breeze or a sound anywhere. Dense. Even the casuarinas trees did not whisper.

    'Anna, are you awake?' Luz asked.
    'Yes – course I am. Can't sleep – can you?'

'No – but I'm not tired – not yet.' Luz switched on the light.

'What about the mosquitoes, Luz? They'll come in through the netting won't they? They always do.'

'You are right, Anna. And anyway it's pointless – there's no air outside either.' Luz shut the window and turned up the fan.

'That's better.' Their cotton nighties flew and billowed up showing thin brown legs on white sheets. They both laughed softly. Neither spoke. They felt the cooling air dry their damp hair. Relief. Luz spoke first.

'Anna – can I ask you something?'

'Of course – as long as it isn't too complicated – it's too late and too hot for that!' Anna smiled in the dark . 'What is it?' she asked.

'It's about Papa. Don't you find he has changed lately? These last few weeks. He's different – he is...' She stopped.

'In what way?' Anna asked immediately.

'Oh, I can't quite explain – even to myself. Just not the same.' Luz sat up. She drew her knees up and hugged them. 'He doesn't laugh anymore – surely you must have noticed that? Something is wrong. I just know it.'

Anna thought carefully.'No,' she said slowly. 'No, Luz, I don't think I have noticed a change. Although, perhaps a little tired maybe. But that's all.' She was satisfied with what she said, totally honest in her opinion. She knew that Luz worshipped her father. 'He does work so hard,' she added. 'And he never complains does he? Have you spoken to your mama, Luz?'

Luz shook her head vigorously. 'No. No, I can't possibly do that – I feel so sorry for her, not myself. But yes, Anna, you are right, Papa does work hard – but then he always has.' She stopped to think, then went on, 'No, it's not work, Anna – it's just that he daydreams all the time; surely you've noticed that? I talk to him and he doesn't answer. It's awful and strange – because it is not Papa. I don't know...' she ended miserably.

Anna listened carefully. She too sat up now, her knees beneath her chin. She said decisively, 'Ask him, Luz. Tomorrow. Ask him straight out – just say what is wrong. You know how he adores you. He will tell you if he's worried about anything. I know he will. Perhaps he even longs for one of you to do that.'

But Luz shook her head. In the dim light Anna could see her black hair cascade and ripple all over her thin shoulders. Silky and snake-like. She turned to Anna. 'Won't you? Ask him? Please, Anna, please. I know you are the right person...'

'Me?' Anna gasped. 'Are you mad? I couldn't. It would be very rude.'

'Please.' Caramel eyes implored her. Impassioned. Anna sighed. She understood that a matter like this was best dealt with straight away. Her mother had taught her that. But who was she to approach this man, the kindest she had ever known? They were not related and really, on reflection, she hardly knew him. It would be insolent – what on earth would he think? He'd probably be angry. She'd never seen him cross – not once – but this... Wasn't she too young anyway? No. It was not her place.

Luz got up suddenly and came over to her bed. She caught Anna's hand and squeezed it so hard it made her wince. 'You will, won't you? I can see you will – oh Anna.' And she bent to kiss her. 'You are like my sister,' Luz told her simply. 'My family love you so much.'
Unexpected tears filled Anna's eyes. 'Alright,' she said. 'I'll try.'

'Promise?'

'Promise – now we must try to sleep.'

As it happened, Juan came to her the very next day. He found her sitting in front of one of the little puestos. She had her easel and paints before her and she sat on a canvas seat. Absorbed. It was hot.

'I knew I would find my English daughter here,' he said. She looked up and there he stood before her.

'I didn't hear you,' she said – completely at ease.

'That's because I'm a puma. I prowl silently and generally in the dark.' He laughed and the sound artificially dispelled last night's worries.

'It's siesta time,' she told him. 'Why aren't you asleep?'

'Why aren't you?' he replied. 'I can't – not today anyway.' He stood quietly by her. He studied her painting, watching all she did attentively. After a long silence, he said,

'Hmm. Pequeña (little one) you have a talent – you really do.'

'Do you honestly think so?' Anna was thrilled. No one had yet seen any of her work.

'I really do. I love your colours. You are very observant – quite unusual for someone your age.' His words patted her back.

'Thank you,' she said. He clapped his hands.

'Next we must have a family portrait. What do you think? Could you manage that? You know the sort I mean. The likeness is captured but we all look ridiculous and stiff at the same time. You do know, don't you? England must be simply littered with them!' He laughed happily. 'You look at them, step back, look again and then you try not to laugh. Instead you think of something madly polite to say about it.' Anna laughed now. She knew exactly what he meant.

'Well?' he asked. 'What do you think – could you manage that?'

'I could try. I'd love to.' Anna thought carefully. The idea was very exciting. 'Yes. Yes. I'll paint you all, if you like.'

'Course I like. We all like.' He laughed again. 'I won't disturb you if I sit down, will I? Will your artistic temperament allow that or will you throw a tantrum and hit me with that rather long paintbrush? Or take my eye out perhaps? Which will it be, Anna?' He did not wait for a reply. He sat down and tilted back his hat.

'I'm glad to see you are wearing one too,' he said. Anna did not stop what she did. She had a brush behind her ear and one in her mouth. She poured water into a little jar and then started to mix colours. Talking was difficult. Juan did not stop. He told her that the puesto before them had been built by his grandfather in about 1870. Built to withstand climate, time and change. He added, rather curiously, that houses like these never fell. Not even in hurricane winds.

'Unlike us.' he concluded quietly. She looked at him then. His voice had changed. He had removed his hat and now fidgeted with the brim with agitated fingers. Anna noted his unease. She heard him whistle tunelessly between clenched teeth. Should she say something? He turned to her, suddenly.

'Anna – Anna – I must speak to you. I – I – need your help.'

'Help?' She was puzzled.

'Yes. Say you will – you will help me. Say yes – now.' She stared down at his face. She saw torment. Gone was the jovial man – the sweetness, the charm. Anna did not recognise him. She looked away not wanting him to see her confusion. She would not fail him. How could she when he had given her so much? She took a deep breath and prepared herself.

'I'm young – but I will try to understand; and help. What is the matter – what can I do?'

With incredible speed, he was up on his knees. He took both her wrists in his hands. Gratitude suffused his face – he looked more like the man she knew.

'Anna.' He paused. He thought. He deliberated. Finally he blurted,

'Anna. Help me – I'm in love.' Ice fell over her brain – paralysed – she fought to hold his eyes. They were full of tears. 'Oh Anna – you are shocked! I have shocked you – I can see it in your sweet face.' He rubbed her hands between his own, unaware that he hurt her. 'You are so good. Can you forgive me?'

'Of course,' she replied. Her voice small but certain. She was bracing herself for the rest.

Juan struggled. He did not mind showing her how much he suffered; he considered it imperative she should know. He continued, 'This person – woman – she is all I want. I cannot think of anything or anyone else. I need her, Anna, and she needs me.' He released her hands then and with his fist, hit the ground. 'Like this earth needs rain . . . ' He said dramatically. His eyes were wild.

'Who is she?' Anna's voice was clipped, matter of fact. She managed to hide her disgust. She surprised herself. And him.

'Oh my God, Anna – you sound so different . . .'

'So do you.' She met him eye for eye. Adult – brave.

'But you aren't going to chastise me are you, with your Anglo-Saxon logic? Please not. Don't remind me of my governess!' He laughed uncertainly. 'What must you think of me?'

'Do you care?'

Juan looked amazed. 'How can you ask such a question? Of course I care.'

'I love you all.' she told him simply. She wanted to cry – a lump had swollen her throat. She didn't want to hear anymore but she knew she must. 'You have all given me the happiest year of my life. You are a perfect family. How can I ever forget that? I feel . . .' Her voice faltered a little. Gently, Juan took her hand.

'Go on, Pequeña. I am listening.'

'I feel I have found a father in you.' Blue eyes met brown. 'It kills me to hear this. You will destroy everyone – your whole family – and why? For what? Who is this person? How can she do this?'

Juan gave her back her hand. He sat back away from her – calm. 'We met last year, Anna – at a cattle sale actually. I saw her sitting on a wooden fence. She was alone, very independent.' He stopped. And he studied Anna's face intently. 'You have never felt love, have you? No – no.' He waved a hand. 'Don't answer me – I know you have not. I can see from your eyes. But you will one day, and you will remember your Juan.'

Anna could hardly bear to witness the sadness in his face at that moment. It would remain with her forever. 'Don't tell me anymore,' she said. 'Just tell me what it is you want me to do.'

His eyes drilled the ground for a moment then he said, 'I want you to give me an alibi.'

'An alibi – why?' Her heart drummed in fear – the premonition of deceit.

'So that I can meet her.' He swung back. 'Please – just once.'

'Just once will become just twice.' The wisdom flew out of her mouth; she had no idea from where. A silence now separated them – it was not an easy one. She loved this man, but he was disappointing her. Anna had made her decision. 'Forgive me – I cannot and will not help you. I will not be an accomplice. To do so would be to betray your family, myself, and you. In fact, everything I believe in. It's unthinkable. You must do as you think best – and I will try not to think less of you.' She got to her feet then, aware of the frantic beating of her heart. She began to pack up her paints.

'But Anna, does anyone have to know? Why can't we share this little secret? I know I can trust you.' He was in agony. She could see that.

'But I will know,' she said. 'It would not be right – surely you can understand that? Maria and the girls is the most perfect thing in your life – there is no room for anything else. No other life apart from them. How can you be so blind?' She was angry.

'But I suffer, Anna, I suffer. You have no idea how much. Can you understand that?'

'Yes. Yes. You suffer because you are like a ridiculous child who can't have the sweets from the top shelf. Once you got what you wanted, it would only become a burden to you and make you miserable. This is pure vanity. It is nothing else.'

He put his head in his hands. He hid from her. Muffled from the depths, he said, 'So you will not help me, then?'

'I will not. You should never have asked me. It was not right.'

He knew from her voice that it would be useless to plead further. He sulked and said, 'Then I will have to find another way.' Anna zipped her bag and picked up the little canvas seat.

'Do,' she told him. 'That is if you want to make a complete fool of yourself.'

She turned to go. He emerged quickly from his hands.

'Don't go, Anna. Can't you see how upset I am? Anna!' he implored. 'You have done this – I feel even worse now.' She laughed then. He saw her soften and patted the grass.

'Five more minutes?' She smiled. How could she refuse?

'Anna, where does all this wisdom come from? It's astonishing! You are so young but I feel quite afraid of you.' And he smiled at her – the smile she knew so well and understood. She felt better – the danger averted, or at least, delayed.

'You could be any age, Anna, 20 – 30 – 80! Some toothless old woman who holds the wisdom of the world in her hands. Which are you? All these ages, I suspect, bound together by the secret of life.'

She lowered her head; his words humbled her – made her care even more for him and his troubles. She did not tell him that in this last hour she had grown up. The cobwebs of innocence no longer veiled her eyes. He was responsible for this. But what he had just said to her gave her the confidence to go on.

'Juan.' (She did not often use his name.) 'Has no one ever told you, or taught you that suffering refines the soul? Makes you a better person? To give something up is salutary. Happiness is not our birthright, you know.' She paused, he listened. She went on, 'It creates the right balance inside you. It enables you to BE and to BE a proper person – a whole person.'

'Bees sting, Anna.' He was being absolutely serious. 'It hurts – I hurt.' He stabbed the area of his heart with a finger. She nodded acknowledging his pain.

'I know. I know. But only for now,' she told him quietly. 'It will not last – can't you see that?'

A defiant 'No' came back at her.

'What on earth would your mother say to you – if you asked her?'

Juan was aghast. 'My mother? She would kill me! I could never discuss such a matter with her. She thinks I'm perfect.' He sat up a little when he said this. Then he shook his head sadly. 'Are you mad?'

'But you have asked me – an idiotic girl who knows absolutely nothing about life at all.' Yes, she was perplexed.

'Did you think that because of my inexperience that I would agree with you?'

Tenderly, he took her hands. He shook his head. 'No. Of course not.' But she did not listen.

'I suppose you thought this stupid English girl would help you. Help you commit the worst mistake of your life. Well, it was not right you know. I would never do anything that would jeopardise your family. Their trust. I'd never be devious.'

His eyes were lit with warmth. He saluted her – she was incorruptible. After a short silence, he sighed and said, 'My God! I think you are a priest!' And they both laughed in united relief. It dispelled all hint of animosity. 'Oh Anna – was there every such a girl. I wonder how you will treat your husband? You have made me feel like a small boy – how do you manage that?'

She smiled openly at him then and said, 'That's because you ARE a small boy. There! You have said it yourself.

You've admitted it. Ha! Now I have an advantage – and it gives me the right to tell you exactly what you are going to do.' She spoke the truth. She did just then feel a small surge of control

'Mierda!' He swore for the first time ever in front of her. Human. Oddly intimate. Softly, under his breath. 'I will listen to you, Anna, but I cannot promise to obey. Be forewarned. And don't be too unkind to me!' He looked wicked – but he looked happier. Less struck down. He was beginning to enjoy himself.

'Well.' Anna pursed her lips together and thought a moment. She stared at the grass.

'No parables, please,' Juan said. 'I couldn't stand it.'
Anna shook her head and agreed with him.

'Course not,' she told him. 'Quite simply this . . .' She paused. It was imperative she get it right the first time. She had to save him. 'Lie down – on your back.'
He did – and so did she. Her head not far from his.

'Now close your eyes – tight.' He did., 'Now count to five.'
He did. Out loud. 'One – two – three – four – five.'

'Now – open them wide.' He did.

'Now!' She snapped her fingers. 'What do you see?'

'Blue sky, of course – what else, you silly girl. Just blue sky, the same colour as my English daughter's eyes. Did you expect me to say Father Christmas?'

'Sh! Concentrate.' Anna tapped his arm sharply. 'Describe what you see – properly. Go on!'
His eyes, always so alert, scanned the blue above him.

'I see the purest blue in or above God's earth. It's fathomless. Without end. No beginning either. Just there all around us. Omnipresent. It's a sort of support, I suppose.' He paused to look at her briefly. 'How am I doing?' Then his eyes returned to the scrutiny. 'Just imagine, Anna, if there was no sky – a huge blank. Wouldn't that be terrifying? I believe it could send one mad.'

'Why?' She crossed her fingers – they were getting there. He, the sheep dog, she, the shepherd.

'Because there would be no boundaries – just an endless gaping vacuum that would swallow us all up.' he gasped quietly. 'Ugh! It's too awful to contemplate. Just imagining it fills me with panic – don't you agree, Anna? Just think! Nothing and more nothing – a hollow absence – no blue anywhere!'

'What colour would there be?' she asked quickly.

'Black, I suppose …Yes, that's what it would be, black as the devil. A beastly frightening thought.'

She watched him intently. Her clear, sweet face focussed encouragingly on him. She felt her heart rise up in her chest – it swelled her throat – now was the moment! The culmination of her little master plan. 'What on earth, compares to that? I mean what could be as terrifying – to you?' She saw him frown. He did not avert his gaze from the sky.

Slowly, he said, 'An empty house. My family gone. A daughter kidnapped; it can happen you know. My wife. . . ' He hesitated. 'My wife, Maria – taken from me – by another man. Alone. To be alone would make me desperate. Yes. That would be my definition of black. That would be my torture.' He answered her very concisely, his thoughts spoken like a list.

Anna was quick to ask, 'And how would they feel if you left? Your darling girls and Maria?'

Silence fell like a lid on them both. A thud that brought conclusion. Anna had difficulty controlling her breathing. It seemed unnaturally loud. Juan reached for her then. His fine and sensitive hand stole over the grass and took hers. She held it firmly in her own. People have been saved by such a hand. Yes!

The sun was losing its warmth. The day was altogether gentler. The intense afternoon heat now allowed a cool breeze to fan it. A sigh of relief went over the land and infiltrated every living thing. Animals visibly relaxed and strolled in matey groups to troughs. Men whistled as they finished a day's work. They threw water over their horses' backs before releasing them into the dusty sunset. Mothers washed children beneath the pumps. They lit fires outside to cook the evening meat. They waited for their men. Dogs stopped panting.

On flat land voices and laughter are carried in acoustic perfection. It is often hard to gage the distance of hooves hitting grassy ground, a man singing in the night – the hoot of an owl – so acutely are sounds picked up and carried over this limitless stage of flatness.

Juan's three girls broke the trance of their quiet. Like Indians they rode bareback and fast. Anna heard them first – quickly, she pulled her hand away from Juan's. She sat up, got to her feet and resumed her original job of packing up her paints. Her soul sang within her – she felt her face must show it.

'Papa! We have been looking for you everywhere! Mama has been going mad.'

Isabel swung off her sweating horse. She looked at her father, mystified. 'What are you doing?' she asked. She looked at Anna who said nothing.

Maria Marta was astonished to find him here. 'What are you doing?' She echoed her sister's words – slightly more dramatic. Only Luz said nothing. She sunk to the ground beside him and put her thin brown arms around his neck.

'Papa,' she said softly. 'Mi Papa.'

'My amazons!' he cried, getting to his feet. 'You have discovered you father doing nothing. Wasting a whole afternoon with his English daughter. You would not believe the things she has been telling me – outrageous!' His daughters looked puzzled.

'Your father has learnt so much in one afternoon – all good things.' He looked over their heads to glance at Anna and she met him with a steady messenger's look. He understood. She saw his face was clear. She stood and watched him hold his girls to him, like a huge bunch of flowers – his arms the ribbon that held them together. The three girls powerful in their need of him – and he intensely vulnerable because of it. Anna was perplexed by her impressions.

'And where is your mama?' he asked the tilted faces. 'Shall we go and find her. We must tell her that Anna is going to paint us – a family portrait! So we must all decide what to wear so we can all look equally ridiculous and important at the same time! And when the portrait is finished we can hang it on the most prominent wall in the house – so no one can ignore it. And we can laugh about it every time we walk passed it.' His daughters were silent. 'Well, what do you think?' They looked at one another; they did not know if he was being serious, even Luz – but they did not care. What mattered was that he was back with them.

Anna watched them walk away – each girl led her horse. Luz turned to wink at her. Anna gave a little nod. They took their father home. She heard their light laughter and chatter, his above the rest. Steady, certain, untroubled.

Anna left two months later. She resisted persuasion to stay. It had to end – her year away. She had grown and she had learnt so much. Maria Acevedo, normally so reserved, held her for some moments before putting her at arm's length, an elegant hand on each shoulder. Her brown eyes beautiful with feeling.

'Never divert from your course, Anna – once you have found it,' she told her solemnly. Then she kissed her forehead. 'Thank you for everything. May God bless you and your mother.' She kissed her again. 'You will find Juan in his office. He is not happy about you leaving us.' And she smiled in a way that lit her whole face and made it luminous with goodness. Anna had been dreading this moment more than any other. But as she walked along the endless corridor, she pulled herself together.

Juan was writing in a large black book but he stopped the moment he saw her. He threw down his pen.

'Ah, here she is – ready to leave us.' He jumped up and opened his arms to her. He embraced her and she put her head against his chest for one brief moment. She would not cry.

'Are you ready?' he asked. 'All packed?' She nodded.

'I am.' Then, 'Will you ever come to England, do you think?'

'Me? Oh what a question!' He frowned; she could see amusement playing around his mouth. 'I don't know, Anna – how does one have to behave there?' Then he laughed as usual. She stood away to look at him.

'As you do here, of course,' she told him simply. 'It's no different. Really.'

'Oh but it is! Much more serious, much too organised. And there is no sun! I think people would find us shocking, don't you? We make too much noise, laugh too much and eat far too late. We never get up in the morning and we are never on time anywhere!' He folded his arms and looked at her. These simple facts stated so much truth on the north and south divide. Juan, unaware of this, merely fought to be light and happy. In reality he wanted to cry. He loved his English girl. He would never forget her. His eyes told her as much.

'You always get up early.' she told him. 'And I'm sure you are never late for anything – ever.'

'That may be,' he acknowledged. 'But we are basically lazy, Anna.' He looked at her, his head on one side.

'I will come to your wedding, Anna,' he said, like a vow. 'I promise.' Solemnly.

'You will?' Anna stared happily at him. 'All of you? How wonderful!' He raised a hand.

'That is if you can find someone brave enough to marry you – it may be difficult.' Anna beamed at him.

'Thank you. Thank you for everything.' He shrugged and said,

'Go now, darling Anna. Quickly. Your car is waiting to take you to the port.' He turned from her now so she no longer saw his face.

'I will see you all again very soon.' She addressed his back. Suddenly the reality of leaving overwhelmed her. She left the room and ran down the corridor. Her rope-soled shoes hitting the polished wooden floor until Juan no longer heard them.

Anna had left England an innocent naïve young girl. She now returned still innocent but not naïve. Wisdom was now in-built. She had learnt so much of human fallibility and the fragile resolve that is open to temptation.

Fernando decided he'd teach his wife a lesson. And Mr. Carr too, come to that.

He watched Sol at the embassy as she circulated from group to group. She was popular and everyone was charmed, amused and enthralled by her. From across the room men surveyed her as they might a work of art – what the eye beheld was pure visual pleasure. Some edged their way through the cocktail crowd to get closer. Fernando enjoyed their tactics – the naked admiration that lit their eyes. He simply adored the idea of other men lusting after his young wife. He always had. It gave his ego a delicious boost and reinforced the primitive right of ownership. She was his and a long time ago he had stamped a DO NOT TOUCH label on her forehead. Just then, a flicker of anger shadowed his eyes – for only a fleeting second; his mouth maintained the social smile throughout. He too moved about the room. He recognised absolutely everyone – or pretended to. His manners did not desert him for one moment.

'Are they really married?' someone asked, hiding her mouth behind a glass, thus making the indiscretion more obvious.

'Oh yes, and have been for years.'

'But he's so old – and she's so lovely.'

'Hmm. But they are devoted; it seems to work very well.' Pause.

'He's very rich, you know.' The woman nodded. A knowing look that said, 'I see' consumed all her facial features. Then she said, 'Yes. Women are whores when it comes to money. We'll do anything.'
They both laughed then – tired, cynical, worldly.
Fernando ate a final olive then moved agilely to collect his wife. He slid an affectionate arm around her waist and with a tender look, 'Come on, my darling girl. It's time to leave.' He gave everyone standing around her his most disarming smile. Immediately she obeyed. Mid-sentence she turned and followed him out.

At dinner they discussed tomorrow. He told her that he'd had to change his plans. Could she go down to Mr. Carr without him? Take the money and bring back the contract. He could not accompany her because he had to be in the city. Would she be all right without him? Yes. Yes, of course she'd be fine. Their driver would look after her. She'd be back by five. Fernando smiled benevolently all the time. Inwardly, he could hardly conceal his glee. What a plan! This would show her who was boss. Sol smiled too. Beneath her cocktail dress, she felt her body glow. They'd be alone! Again.

As she fell asleep, she planned what she'd wear to look her very best. Side by side – and separate – the couple thought about the next day. But one was victor and the other – victim. It was fortunate indeed that Sol could not see the diabolical grin on her husband's face. Nor he the bliss that had settled like dew on hers.

True darkness protected them both from the other.

Tomorrow became today. And above the sound of gushing taps, Fernando heard his wife singing.

Anna heard the same. Johnny was having his bath too. He was a different man from the one twenty-four hours ago. Literally, she felt a tired grey winter skin had been peeled away and beneath there sparkled new growth. Cool, fresh, supple, baby-pink. Ten years cast off overnight. Anna allowed herself a little sense of triumph. Patience had paid off – so had prayer. Her sweet face shimmered with relief. To see Johnny so happy made her heart sing. It was the moment she had longed for – and now it was here – today. She watched him emerge from the bathroom, her hero, still singing as he dressed. 'You could sell me anything,' she murmured, more to herself than to him.

'What?' he called, 'Are you talking to yourself?'

'Of course. There's no one else in bed with me.' Anna gazed at him. Happy. So happy.

'I shan't be late today.' He leant over her. Kissed her forehead. Brushed back her hair with his fingers. Kissed her again. 'I'm off.'

She stood by the window and watched him drive away. A lovely sunny morning held the voluptuous promise of a perfect day. Dressing quickly, she went downstairs, and flung open every window. She wanted to be out in her garden.

'Postman!' It was Bert banging on the open door. 'There's a registered for you, Mrs. Carr. Could you sign please?'

'Bert – morning to you.' Anna appeared from the kitchen. 'What a lovely day – you must hate being in your van, don't you?'

'You look well, Mrs. Carr. May I say I haven't seen you looking so cheerful for a very long time.'

'Thank you, Bert. I feel cheerful.' She smiled at him. He handed her the post, the registered one lay on top.

'Sign here, please, Mrs. Carr.' And he pointed to the dotted line. She scribbled her name rapidly – she was impatient to be out. 'Great. See you soon.'
Sometimes he came in for a cup of tea. She was thankful that today he seemed to be in a hurry. She walked to the kitchen and tore open the registered one – the others could wait.

Her eyes scanned the page before her. At first, she did not understand what she read. She sat down and read it again. She let out a small gasp, ran her hand through her hair, looked up and stared ahead of her, then back to the page. What she read began to overwhelm her. She put the letter down on the table, covered her face with her hands and started to cry. Her shoulders trembled very slightly. Suddenly she sat up, composed herself and with a resolute air walked to the telephone. She rang Victoria. 'Come now.' she said. 'Straight away if you can – I've got something I must tell you.'

'Course.' said Victoria, from her desk. 'I'll be with you in fifteen minutes. Are you alone? Are you alright?'

'I am. I am,' said Anna. She now had a little smile on her face.

Sol thought she might burst if the car did not go faster. She had never felt like this before. This new feather-light sensation of floating was indescribable. She was like a giddy young girl, flushed and unprepared, wanting two more hours with this man. With that, she felt she'd gain the world and feel the essential primeval beat that was the core to all life. She wanted the secret of her being to be pierced, shattered and then restored – returned to her in a completeness she had never known. Love, up till now had been a polite – reserved – duty. Now, she was wild. This was her moment – a secret she would hold inside her all her life. As she was seduced, so she would seduce.

She brushed her hair, re-painted her lips – poppy-red – creamy olive skin – black hair above an ice-blue silk shirt. She wore little gold leopard cuff links, that matched her earrings. Her driver, George, watched her from his mirror. He had been paid to do this. He noted her excitement, her preparation. It filled his car.

'Another ten minutes, Mrs. La Costa. We are bang on time.'

She smiled, her lovely liquid eyes meeting his in the little mirror that was his spy.

'Of course.' She nodded. 'Thank you, George. You always do time our arrivals down to the last second – that's because you are English.' She laughed lightly. He nodded. Proud to be so. He did not say that if people where she came from cared to look at their clocks more often, their countries might be a lot more organised. None of this mañana business for him, thank you very much. Time for George was law. Without G.M.T. he'd go mad.

'Here we are.' He rounded into the driveway. Sol sat very upright on the edge of the seat, a hand on the door. Johnny opened it before George could get round. It was an affront to his profession. A chauffeur always opened the door.

The couple disappeared rapidly inside the office. Sol handed him the sealed envelope. Johnny took it and put it on his desk.

'Sol.' he said. 'this can go no further. You know that, don't you?'
She looked at him and was pleased to see he battled. She would not let this go. She wanted only this day, nothing more. And she'd keep it forever cupped against her heart. No one would be harmed, no one would know.

She stepped towards him and he felt himself go weak. Before him was sensual perfection, touchingly unspoilt. She longed for him – it emanated from every part of her – a palpable aura of request. Inwardly, he slumped as his resolve gave way to the blinding desire that was her. She stood beneath him now, she looked up. Softly, she said, 'Just one day, Johnny. That's all.' He stared, mesmerised, at this beautiful face and he put his hands on her fine-boned shoulders.

Anna handed Victoria the letter. She read it carefully – twice. A slow smile of satisfaction spread across her clever face. She looked up.

'Can you believe it yet? It's the most exciting thing I have read in a long time.'
Anna was pale. 'Not yet,' she said. 'I just cannot believe he remembered me. It was so long ago – another life. It's the sort of thing that happens in books, Victoria. You know, the happy ending, everyone saved by a scarcely credible turn of events.' She laughed awkwardly.

'Come on!' Victoria told her. 'Allow yourself some celebration. Where's the champagne?' Her eyes darted around the kitchen, taking in the shabbiness. She could see no bottles. The wine rack was empty. 'You'll be able to get the house done up now,' she said tactlessly. 'You will be able to do exactly what you like, Anna. Imagine that!'
Victoria now stood, with her hands on her hips – her pose triumphant, happy for her friend. 'Buy a picture, a house in Europe, a boat. You name it, you can have it.'

'Don't be idiotic, Victoria. I don't want any of those things – except of course, this old house . . .'

'But how can you possibly know what you do and don't want, Anna, at this early stage? You've never really had anything that you bought for yourself – for your own pleasure. Try it and believe me, you'll soon get the hang of acquiring beautiful things that belong to you.' She saw the doubt in Anna's face so, she said, 'Well, for heaven's sake don't give it all to the church will you?'

'No. No. I certainly shan't do that. But I will see what Johnny feels about it first.'

'Yes. Yes, of course.' Victoria could not disguise the impatience she felt. 'But consider Anna Carr too. You never do and it's bloody well time you did. That's an order!'

'Do you know the saddest thing about all this, Victoria?'

'Sad? Can there be such a thing? What?'
Anna's eyes welled as she said,

'I can't say thank you to him.'
Victoria rummaged for her sympathetic tone while inwardly she was thinking – ' too bad.' 'No, of course you can't.' she said. 'I can see that must be painful.' She did not dare add that it would be a lot more painful without the money. It simply wasn't the moment. For now, the news had a curious lack of joy about it. Not real. But Anna brightened when she said,

'I wonder what the others will think? What will they tell me to do?'

'Not hard to imagine, is it? Honor will tell you to discuss the whole damn thing with Johnny before even considering opening a page of your cheque book – and Smiley – exactly the opposite! She'll book you into a health farm and then take you on a massive shopping spree in London.'

'And you?'

'Me? I'd tell you to be careful. Think long and hard about what you want from life.' Victoria went over to her and quite unexpectedly, hugged her. 'You look so vulnerable, Anna. Is it so terrible to be left a million dollars?' She crouched down by Anna's chair and studied her face with scrupulous attention. She seemed so small just then – surprisingly unworldly. Which of course, she was.

'Don't look so worried, Victoria. I'll get used to it very soon. It's just such a shock! But once I know Johnny has all he needs, I'll decide what else to do.' She thought a moment. The colour was ebbing back into her face. 'In fact, I'm really terribly excited, Victoria. It's absolutely wonderful, isn't it?'

She had Juan's face before her. Utterly real, she felt she might touch it. He stared at her. 'Somewhere I have a photograph of him, of them all.' she told Victoria. 'The kindest person I've ever known. I've told you all about them – so long ago, Victoria, and now this! He called me his English daughter.' Anna smiled at the memory. 'The happiest year of my life in so many ways. I grew up there, I suppose.'

'Always an epic moment in anyone's life.' Victoria assumed the carnal. 'I grew up in Italy, overnight – all very messy and unsuitable, as far as I can remember.'

'No. No, I don't mean that. I simply meant I learnt so much about life in that one year. It sort of formed me.'

'I see. So you boarded the boat *intactus?*'

Anna actually blushed. 'We're not in court, Victoria,' she replied humorously. 'Of course I did.'

'Bravo; though quite how you managed that I'd love to know – another day perhaps. Now. . .' She rubbed her hands together. 'Let's talk about this lovely money. How can I help?' Victoria's indigo eyes changed and took on a professional look. She perched her half-rim glasses on her fine strong nose. Anna knew she was in safe hands.

'Advice,' she said. 'Who else can I trust? I want practical, legal advice. From you.' She prodded Victoria with her finger and the two women smiled at each other. Anna's good fortune was beginning to sink in – her prayers had been more than answered. She had never asked for this.

Johnny stood alone in his office. He was surrounded by a deathly quiet. The day was over, his men had gone. He had only to lock up and go home himself. But. . .
How on earth was he ever going to tell Anna? He could hardly bear to contemplate her disappointment. He winced inside. But as usual, she'd understand – with that saintly fortitude. The certainty of her reaction faintly irritated him. He knew too she'd comfort him using calm, philosophical words. Words that were intended to pat and stroke away his agitation, his failure. Skilfully she would bring him back to the featherbedded safety she always had ready for him. Her unplayed feminine wisdom would prevail and she'd look after them both. But Johnny did not want this. If only she'd fling a teapot at his head. Far better she scream at him, call him a bastard. A lying, cheating bastard. He felt himself worthy of that title. He'd like some passionate response from her – more fishwife than lady.

He did not want to be offered the benefit of the doubt. He did not deserve or want her sweetness and understanding. He wanted fire. But Anna would not do that. It would not be like that.

Sol had gone. Yvonne had left early for a doctor's appointment – or so she had said. The workshop was now closed. Johnny stood by his window in the office. Ridiculously, he re-read Fernando's letter.

'Dear Mr. Carr,

As you see I have decided not to enclose a cheque. My reason being that I do not want to do business with you. You may have the audacity to question why? Let me explain myself. I do not like men who see fit to do business with the husband while pursuing the wife. I'm sure it is not necessary for me to enlarge on this. You will comprehend what I say. You are not a fool. It is a pity, but my wife is more important to me than two Ferraris. I will tell her this when you return her to me.

Fernando La Costa.'

It was with dread that Sol returned. It was with fear that she approached the door of their apartment. Her heart drummed when she saw her husband. He came towards her with apparent pleasure – a broad smile on his face – but as she drew nearer and was but a foot away, he raised his hand and, like lightening, cracked it across her face. She let out a small cry. She felt blood fill her mouth. She held her lips together to contain it. Her eyes smarted with tears.

'That's what you get, my dear, for making a fool of your husband.' His eyes shimmered with fury. 'There will be no car and no Mr.Carr for you. Do you understand? And take that ridiculous look of surprise off your face – it does not suit you. Do you think that I'm some sort of fool?'

Sol sobbed, holding her mouth against a handkerchief. The vivid stain of red seeped over it. Her day and the radiance it had given her vanished and was replaced by a wretchedness so acute that she wanted to die. Had she been able to instrument her end then, she would not have thought twice. Fernando grabbed her hair and forced her head back. She thought she might choke.

'Have I made myself clear?' he asked. 'Answer me!' And while he waited for a reply, he feasted on his little sadistic triumph. Sol could only whimper – she was utterly powerless to defend herself. Her knees crumpled – not in contrition – and she slumped onto the sofa behind her. Several strands of her black hair remained in Fernando's clenched hand. 'That's right. You need a rest.' His sarcasm whipped her. 'Stay here while I make a phone call.'

'To whom?' she managed to ask feebly. Did she care? It was painful to speak through swollen lips.

He smiled and completed his revenge saying, 'Who do you think? To Mrs. Carr of course. She will be surprised, won't she? There are a few things I think she should know.'

His words plunged the final sword between her shoulder blades, destined to pierce her heart. She saw it was pointless to plead; to do so would be to admit guilt. Sol would never do that. What did it matter anyway? What did anything matter now?

She lay back against the cushions, shocked, tired and dreadfully sad. Her little foray into love was now far away. A glazed memory in fact – not a part of her anymore. Another life obliterated beneath the cruelty of Fernando's hand.

In the following months, she spent many hours alone. She analysed over and over again what had happened. She refused to discuss any part of it with friends. They saw the hurt – her loss of weight, the bitten nails. They noted the sadness that now seemed permanently settled around her eyes. She was nervy, withdrawn – often far away. Inaccessible. Eventually the journey of her private thoughts healed her. She concluded that passion was highly dangerous. A futile explosion of emotion that could send you mad and worse, a loss of oneself. A blind tumbling into unbalanced terror.
She could not get rid of her guilt. It hung around her like some dreadful symptom she could not cure. It hampered Sol. She wanted more than anything in the world to return to herself – to be allowed once more to touch all things familiar. To the wonderful clean simplicity of her child. She'd never be tempted again. It had done nothing for her. Johnny's arms had not liberated her. The blinding release, once over, had not made her evolve into a lasting private freedom of her own. Instead, like some cautious animal that scents danger, she stepped back. It suited her to believe that she had wholly deserved her husband's brutality, both physical and verbal. It gave her the limits

she needed and understood. Those moments, the brief duration of bliss had contained a whole life. But like a galaxy of shooting stars, the intensity was but an eye blink in time. And afterwards an emptiness so acute, so desolate she felt that people must surely see the gaping void that emanated from every pore.
She sought reality – reality provided sense and sense equalled order and sanity. She'd settle for that.

But Fernando died. He had so debilitated her self-confidence that life without him terrified her. She had nothing to set her day by. It was a crisis she resolved by becoming neurotic. And then she became reclusive, and then, in the natural order of healing – she recovered.

She began to paint. She became successful. She did not need the outside world. Her imagination flew and she produced outstanding work. An artist of note and something of a myth as she was rarely seen. There was now nothing to jeopardise her progress – nothing between her and the sky. Her favourite subject of limitless possibility. The cosmic sphere, her canvas; her paints and brushes the release of anguish.

She relied on her son and his family for human contact. Luca adored his mother and although now married, he never found a woman to match her. Sol loved them all and drew great strength from the continuity of life they represented. She knew her son was consistently unfaithful but she said nothing. Life had taught her to keep her mouth shut and maintain a façade of absolute discretion. The world was full of Johnny Carrs and her son was one of them. It was woman's role to create harmony, no matter what. Women were not supposed to break out and seek illicit pleasure. Their place was in the home – in a position of pedestalled reverence. The macho culture won out every time. Few women thrived outside its rules. Sol instilled this in her grandchildren. As she spoke these words she was taken back to what had been her private hell. Now completely restored, she could not believe that woman had been her. Her grandchildren sat before her spellbound. They filed away every word she said to them.

Their grandmother was their oracle.

Anna visibly froze on hearing Johnny's car in the drive.

'I'll go.' Victoria offered. She was livid with him.

'No – no.' pleaded Anna. 'Stay, please don't leave me. Just sit. Be normal.'

'How?' Victoria spat back.

Enter the sinner quite unaware of their knowledge. Anna smiled – so did Victoria – in league. They got to their feet, both women kissed him.

'Let's have a drink; all of us.' From Anna. She marched to the fridge, pulled the handle with notable energy and got out the ice. 'Victoria – what will you have?'

Victoria, sensing the storm ahead, wanted to leave. The showdown was imminent. Anna announced battle in her movements. With great purpose, she almost ran about the kitchen collecting glasses, nuts, tonics. Anger seemed to rise up from her. She was poised, her dagger drawn. Johnny looked bemused. He was silent and watched everything. He felt the sea change but could not fathom the source – did she know? How could she know?

'I'm off – must go.' Victoria picked up her bag. She slung it over her shoulder decisively. She was careful not to look at Johnny. He could hardly disguise his relief. He wanted to get the next bit of torture out of the way.

'Bye – I'll ring you tomorrow, Anna.' With meaning. She left.

'How long has she been here?' he asked. Anna noticed his attempt to sound buoyant.

'All day, pretty well – why do you ask?'

'That's not like her is it? I mean for Victoria work is more important than any other thing.'

Johnny poured himself a drink. He took a huge gulp, then added more gin.

'What about me? Are you going to ask me what I'd like to drink?' Anna could not disguise the clip in her voice. She watched this man – her husband – now so safe. He may have wide athletic shoulders, she thought, but it was she who carried the weight. How dare he! How dare he now humiliate her? Lightly, she managed to say,

'Well – and has your day ended as you'd hoped? Is the bank over-flowing with money?' Her eyes pierced his back. Her throat drummed, unable to swallow. She felt a sort of rising sensation that could overwhelm her – it came from her stomach and was unfamiliar. Rage fuelled her anguish. Powerful. She felt she could faint.

'Well?' she asked again when he did not respond. More silence.

'Anna.' he said finally and very quietly. From where she stood, she could scarcely catch his words. 'Anna. It's off. It's finished – the business – this – house. Me.' Stunned, exhausted – spent. He turned then and looked at her. A dazed abstract expression in his eyes. Gone was the peaceful, patient man. A broken one. Anna could not meet his eyes. Mr. LaCosta had not told her this. Only the infidelity. With a devil's skill, he'd left it to Johnny to tell her. His revenge came full circle – they were now both knocked off their feet. Anna's legs felt weak; she supported herself against the cupboards. Wounded now, she forgot her own good fortune.

'I will tell the children.' he went on quietly. 'Then I will go away for a few days.'

'Away? Where to?'

'God knows. I just need to be alone now. I need to think. I can't do that here.' He emptied his glass and poured another.

'But this is your house, Johnny . . .'

'Not for much longer,' he cut in curtly.

Anna felt panic seep through her. She was losing him. She was certain of it. She remained outwardly steady. 'When - when do you think you will come back?'

He looked at her then. 'I can't say.'

'You are being cruel, Johnny. At least tell me where you'll be – you always have before. It is the very least you can do.'

'Why should I? I'm finished, Anna. The last thing you need is a useless bloody man round your neck.'

'Oh for God's sake, Johnny – don't feel so bloody sorry for yourself.'

'You are right. I do feel sorry for myself, and it's not a pleasant feeling. But frankly I can't think of any other right now.'

'You're tired,' she told him reasonably, the tone of voice he dreaded.

'Course I am.' He flung back angrily. His face now furrowed with the blows of the day. 'What the hell do you expect me to be?'

Anna felt checkmated. What was there to say right now? Johnny had spent the day with another man's wife. And now he had come home guilty and bankrupt.

'Alright.' she said. 'Go – but not for long – five days. We'll talk when you get back.'

She walked over to him then and kissed his cheek. She left him standing stiffly in the kitchen. He did not try to touch her but she thought she heard him say, 'Anna – Anna.' Very softly as she left the room.

Anna fled to their bedroom. Anger had given way to fear. She fell on the bed trembling. The day that had begun with a flaming torch blazing with promise, now ended ash-grey about her. Empty. Bleak. Betrayal.

She lay on her back dreading the oncoming darkness. She watched the rose-hued sky fade and vanish. Paralysed in black silence, her world had gone cold and numb. She knew she should get up and move but just then she thought it would be lovely to die. Why not?

The door clicked open. It made her jump. Quickly she closed her eyes. Johnny moved quietly about the room. She heard him pull clothes out of the cupboard – take his bedside clock. He went to the bathroom and she heard him unzip his old leather sponge bag. He returned to their room and for a few seconds stood silently. She knew he watched her. She said nothing but made herself breathe in the regular rhythm of deep sleep. It was the stuff of old films. He turned and quietly left the room. She heard him on the stairs – the hall – the front door. The car. She sprang off the bed then and rushed to the window. In time to see the rear lights of the car disappear. He was gone. A throbbing silence engulfed her. Her life spun out of control. She was now in open sea – no rudder, no oars and no Johnny.

But a new day came. Life fluttered its wings and petals in her garden. The scent of honeysuckle wafted into the room. The air, so fresh and pure brought a clean optimism through the window. Anna lay, ball-like and still dressed in yesterday's clothes. She moved and felt stiff. She stretched and was aware that reality would hit her the moment she opened her eyes. So she hung on to eye-lid darkness while feeling the light all about her. She evaded the confrontation of it and all that it would bring. Slowly, she prepared herself. She knew she would need an almighty strength to get through this day. She planned a bath. It would thaw her out, comfort her, and give her back a degree of dignity and normality. She'd dress in clean clothes, wash her hair. She'd go down to the kitchen, let the animals out. She'd have breakfast and then …what would she do then? What did other women do at that hour when they had been left? Did they wait? Wait for the telephone? Endure the torture of silence. A ridiculous and futile exercise.

As her senses surfaced and lost their sleep, she remembered her inheritance. A flutter of genuine excitement rushed through her. A million dollars! What on earth was that in pounds? Victoria would know. She'd ring her after breakfast. A mini-plan. It gave her a little lift of energy. She opened her eyes and sat up. The sun met her and she smiled back at it. Everything was going to be all right – surely.

'Men and their dicks!' said Smiley scornfully. 'I can't honestly say I'm surprised.'

'Yes – well – you might at least find a better way of expressing it; this is Anna we are talking about.' Honor said with disdain. Victoria had told them of Johnny's behaviour.

'No, it's not, Honor – you are wrong. We have Johnny on the slab here, not Anna,' retorted Smiley. 'There IS no other way to talk about it. Facts are facts – these stink – face it! That three piece suite is the cause of more trouble than anything else on earth. Men really are bastards.' Smiley mixed anger with humour. She found the wrong done to Anna difficult to deal with. Honor looked horrified. She was not in the mood to joke. Infidelity was an anathema to her. She adored Anna, admired her and she could not laugh at something that was so profoundly awful. She'd stand by her – absolutely – in her hour of humiliation and need.

Oh God! If Gerald did this to her! She was certain she'd find the highest building in Winchester and fling herself off it.

'She'll be here soon, Smiley. For heaven's sake don't talk like that in front of her, will you?'

'Do you honestly think that I would? Course I won't! Poor love. No one feels more sorry for her than I do. It must be utter hell for her.' Smiley looked rueful. 'Oh look – here she is! From their table they watched Anna thread her way towards them. Victoria was with her. Smiley leapt to her feet and hugged her. Honor followed suit though was not so effusive. She squeezed Anna with heartfelt funereal sincerity and said quietly, 'Hello, Anna.'

'Good to see you, Anna.' from Smiley. You look great.' she lied.

'No I don't, I look like hell,' Anna retorted coolly. Smiley's eyes told her that she agreed. Victoria coughed behind her and said,

'Anna – aren't you going to tell them your news?' She arched her fine eyebrows and inclined her head in query.

'News? What news?' asked Honor.

'We know it already,' offered Smiley accommodatingly.

'No, you don't.' Victoria informed her sharply. 'Come on, Anna.'

They all sat down. The restaurant was packed for lunch. A real mix of people. Women, like themselves, up for the day; Knightsbridge shoppers and young businessmen and girls. Conversation buzzed to a level pitch all around them. It was enjoyable and Anna felt wonderfully anonymous. She shouted her news at the top of her voice and well above the row. It released some of the fury she held within her. Today she was angry. Yesterday she had been fearful, wretched like an animal that seeks the forest on being shot. She peered out with bleary, blood-shot eyes and a thumping heart. She hated everything and everyone, including herself. But today, anger. Much better. Positive and strong. Tomorrow, who knew? She could not control how she'd feel. Lying on this bed of chaos made every future second unpredictable. Instinctively she prepared herself for a walk through minefields.

'A million dollars! I don't believe it.'

'Wonderful!' Smiley grinned from ear to ear.

'Victoria is now my official adviser.' Anna patted Victoria on the back. Then she delved into her bag to find the letter of proof. They all had their eyes on her face. They all had a smile on their lips.

'Right!' Smiley was the first to speak. She hit the table with her glass. 'Shopping spree! New everything, Anna. New you. How about it? Let's start today – after lunch.'

'Humph. Whatever for?'

'Why ever not, you mean. Come on.' Smiley tried to conceal her exasperation.

'Let's all have a bloody Mary,' she said. 'And let our imaginations rip.' She saw the continued doubt in Anna's face 'Heavens! It's not every day that someone leaves you that sort of money.'

Honor said nothing. She was thinking long and hard about poor Anna's situation. She took a deep breath and said, 'Keep it for a rainy day, Anna. You have no idea what the future holds.'

'A monsoon I should think,' said Anna dryly. 'You are right though, Honor.' She touched her arm in thanks. Smiley handed her a large drink. She took several gulps. And very soon felt the uplifting effects of midday drinking. Quite unused to it, she became rapidly enveloped in a paradoxical oblivion – lucid as a barn owl at midnight but removed from her reality. Perfect!

Voices barked all around her. She gazed out from her comfortable chair. A spectator. She watched the human race celebrating life. She heard wild laughter, saw male hands stroking narrow female shoulders. She watched those insistent hands gently massaging towards the waist and further. She saw thin girls lean comfortably against their men. Two halves becoming one whole – temporarily. Mesmerised, Anna tingled. She was absolutely fascinated by all she saw. Country life certainly did not offer this moving collage of life. Hands, teeth, darting eyes, movement sitting down, standing up – laughter; giddy enjoyment here, there, and everywhere. Whirling transitory joy. The lunch hour that snatched at much more than food. It spun all about her – like the big wheel at...

'Anna! You are looking pale. Are you going to be sick?'
They did not wait for a reply. They all jumped together to their feet. Flanking her, they hurried through the people and found the bathroom.

'Good Lord! You aren't supposed to be in here. This is the gents.' said a voice.
No longer. The sickness rose in her throat and like a gushing fountain, left her mouth. It splashed everywhere. Anna saw black polished shoes made filthy by her.

'Oh my God.' said the voice. 'You poor woman – what is the matter?'

'She is not feeling well and has been sick.' Victoria informed him in her most matter-of-fact voice.

'I can see that. How dreadful. Let me get her a chair.'

'Please,' said Honor. 'That would be very kind.' She stroked Anna's hair. To her the situation was extremely embarrassing.

'Let's get her out of here – she needs fresh air.' Smiley was right. Between them, they shepherded her out on to the pavement.

'Now breathe deeply,' ordered Smiley. 'One – two – three – that's right.' Anna did exactly what she was told

'That's better – you look better now.'

'Feel better,' Anna told them.

The man now returned with a chair. 'Here, have this,' and he pushed it against the back of Anna's legs making her sit down with a plonk.

'Thank you so much – you really are the kindest person in the world,' she told him weakly. Her eyes scanned his shoes. Distantly she wondered how Johnny would have reacted to some strange woman being sick on him.

'Don't worry about them,' he told her quickly. 'Now, how do you feel?'

He bent to look at her properly. She gazed in to a kind and concerned face.

'Much better.' She was able to smile. 'Too much vodka, you see – not used to it.'

They all laughed then. He stood up, satisfied now that she would be all right, and told them to fetch him if he was needed. The four women thanked him.

When he got back to the bar he was told, 'If you've got to be sick in the gents, sir, please tell us and we'll clean it up. The odour, sir, is quite offensive to our other customers.' He said nothing but shrugged politely.

'I'll have my smoked salmon now, please.'

'Sure that's wise, sir? You really ought to go home and lie down.'

'I'll have it now,' he repeated firmly. And he smiled – more to himself. He was pleased to have come to the aid of such a pretty woman. The sort he admired. Old-fashioned and very gracious too. Characteristics that went hand in hand and were now being eroded by the speed of life. He sipped his drink and while he did so, tried to imagine what her husband might be like. He conjured up a steady, solid man, a library, Labradors; devoted to her of course. Their lives run by the clock that ticked in the hall. Their garden holding the village fete, the lesson read by him every Sunday. He reflected on his own wife. She was attractive, but in a completely different way. Much stronger, more London. In her day, she had been considered a 'looker'. Now, they just knew one another too well – nothing to get excited about. Rather like an old pair of slippers. Monogrammed, of course.

'Bring me some more of that salmon would you, Arthur. And another drink.'

'I knew it! I knew it, Lennie. What did I tell you? That woman. She has brought us all down.'

'Calm down, woman.' Come and sit at the table and have your tea. You'll blow up, if you don't.'
Yvonne obeyed. But she could not eat. 'I shall be sick if I do,' she told him. Beads of sweat appeared all over her face – and yet it was not hot.

'You're in a fair old fret, Yvonne. Now sit still and at least drink some tea.' He poured from the old brown teapot, standing beside her. He patted her back and then returned to his seat. 'Now drink it,' he told her gently. 'Do you good.' Lennie knew the situation was bad because he had heard it all in the pub the night before. He'd said nothing to his wife. Had Mr. Carr bolted? No one seemed to know.

'He hasn't contacted me, Lennie. That's what's worried me the most. He's never done this before. Never.'
Lennie shook his head in sympathy. Her distress reinforced his decision not to repeat pub talk, She would be shocked; the language used was not for her ears. 'He will, love. Let's all calm down – you did leave the answer phone on, of course?' She nodded, deep in thought.

'What if he's dead, Lennie? That woman could do him in, you know. Like a witch. Poor Mrs. Carr. She never deserved this.' Her eyes suddenly brimmed at the thought of Anna. 'She's never harmed anyone, Lennie. And now!

What a mess! There's no money, Lennie. All gone. No orders. Nothing!'

Yes, it certainly was a bad state of affairs – enough to rattle the local community for several months to come. Nothing so thrilling as the whiff of scandal that involved a beautiful woman. It would keep tongues wagging for days. False and accurate assumptions would be made. Only the wise would be silent. And then of course, the entire population would be behind the wife. That poor, ill-treated woman was everyone's idea of a perfect lady. Unobtrusive, kind and always ready to help. She had the knack of getting on with all walks of life. Understated too, but somehow always worthy of consultation. Her opinion mattered – her approval even more. People knew of their financial difficulties but somehow being 'gentry' excluded them from unjust conclusions. A city crash was the most likely explanation for their present misfortune. Both, after all, came from moneyed families. But now this! An altogether different slant cast a shadow on their hitherto exemplary lives. It was beyond belief! Mr. Carr? This charming, steady, church- going man. A family man too, liked by everyone. Well. Well. In the pub it was said he was 'cunt struck.' 'He'll be in touch, love, sooner than you think. Let the man rest awhile. He needs to gather his thoughts – he'll come to his senses soon enough.'

Dear Lennie. So level headed and fair. Yvonne knew that he was usually right about matters of the world. 'Do you really think so, Lennie?' She dabbed her eyes.

'Yes. Yes,' he confirmed. 'I do really think so. I wouldn't say so otherwise. You know that.'

'No one at the house either.'

'No – well she needs a rest too, I dare say. Probably in London with one of the children.'

Yvonne nodded. She got up from the table then and cleared away the tea things. 'I'll wash up later,' she said. 'I've brought home some work which I'll do quickly.'

He nodded patiently realising his wife's distress. The order of her life had been shattered and it upset her deeply. 'Off you go,' he said. 'But don't forget our evening walk.'

She closed the door and Lennie reached for the newspaper. His eyes ran appreciatively over the topless girl – from there he turned to the sports pages.

'I would never wear this – not in a million years.'

Anna stood before a large and unforgiving mirror. On the chair lay a pile of clothes selected for her by Smiley. They had that brand new smell and were very expensive.

'It's far too short, Smiley. Too flashy and too young. Not me.'

'Well okay. What about this?' Smiley held up a dark-blue wrap round skirt with a leafy pattern on the silk.

'Hm. Now that looks better. Let's see.' She slipped it on.

'Now that really is nice,' Smiley approved. 'No – it's not too tight. Don't wriggle.'

Anna smiled. It looked good. She felt good. She liked what she saw. Something rather nice about the feel of silk on the hips.

'How much?' she asked. The assistant looked at the tag that hung behind her.

'£350,' she said solemnly.

'What?' Anna gasped. 'Is it really. I simply can't believe it.'

'That's nothing,' Smiley told her. 'You're only shocked because you haven't shopped for years. All good clothes come with a healthy price tag these days. It's nothing to spend a thousand pounds on a suit, Anna.'

'I can't possibly spend that sort of money on this.'

'Oh go on! Why on earth not? It looks wonderful. And you'll wear it forever.'

The assistant smiled approvingly at Smiley's words. Just the sort of customer she loved. She now handed Anna a shirt.

'This goes with the skirt,' she said.

Anna had to admit, albeit silently that she looked wonderful. Transformed. A little twinge of self-admiration crept over her. It was quite pleasurable.

'Well?' Smiley put her head to one side and looked at her. Her own eyes danced at the fun of it all and the change she witnessed. It had brought a blush to Anna's face.

'You look beautiful,' she told her. 'Take them both. Then let's go and look for some shoes. We can fling those moccasins of yours into the Thames on the way home.'

Anna felt a little wave of excitement take hold of her. She was beginning to enjoy herself. Spending money and the anticipation of spending as much as she liked acted as a temporary cork against her misery. As she handed the clothes to the assistant she decided she'd shop all day, thereby joining the sisterhood of women who daily anaesthetised themselves with this intoxicating activity. It gave them a fix that nothing else on earth could match.

And Smiley was the perfect accomplice. Anna put her arm through hers and the two women left the shop united in purpose.

Three thousand pounds later and in the fading light, they took a taxi back to Smiley's flat. Anna sat on the floor surrounded by boxes and bags that frothed with tissue and were full of beautiful, meaningless things. She was visited by ridiculous guilt. The excess that lay about her suddenly seemed to emphasise the bleakness of her situation. When would she ever use any of these things? She was visibly exhausted, her feet in agony, encased in exquisite Italian shoes. Smiley was visibly the opposite – she was elated. It was a triumph to her that she had got this far with Anna. But now, back in the flat and away from the mesmeric buzz of the shops, Anna felt the glow leave her. She was suddenly angry at the absurdity of her day. Surprised too. She of all people – how could she be so foolish? Vanity! That's all it was. She was harsh on herself – oblivion was a better word. Smiley came towards her bringing two glasses with her. And a big smile.

'Here, have some wine, Anna.' She sat down beside her on the carpet.

'Here's to today. The new you.' And she raised her glass and looked with satisfaction at the surrounding evidence of their day. Anna raised her glass in return, although somewhat half-heartedly.

'It's monstrous,' she said. 'I've spent nearly three thousand pounds. I can't believe it. It's not funny, Smiley.' But Smiley licked her lips.

"Hm. Doesn't it make you feel good?'

'No.' Anna emphatically replied. 'Absolutely not.'

Smiley's face fell a fraction. Quickly Anna rectified,

'Course it's fun and I've loved every minute of it – but – but is this really what women do all the time here? Can't they think of something better to do with their time?'

Smiley thought.

'Well – we are in the world's most exciting city for shops, you know. There's temptation everywhere you look. London has just about everything. And anyway,' she justified, 'Anybody will tell you that people find shopping more fulfilling that anything else.'

'Well, it's monstrous, Smiley.' Anna would not be convinced but she did look more amused.

'What about you? Does it make you happy?' she asked again.

'Happy? God no. It just makes me feel good about myself and that is what is important. Perhaps – perhaps it makes me forget that I'm NOT happy, that my life is a pretty good mess, that basically I'm useless – God knows and who cares?'

Anna frowned. She always enjoyed a discussion. 'Are you being quite serious? Do you really mean that a very intelligent and perceptive person like yourself gets that sort of buzz? That is the right word isn't it – buzz?' Smiley nodded. 'Don't you find it vacuous?' Anna thought it would be rude to say 'empty-headed.'

'A lot of life is vacuous, Anna, you must agree with that,' Smiley answered her with force.

'Some people play tennis, others golf – you paint, you garden – others shop, go to the hairdresser. I don't know – everyone has their own way of finding an outlet for enjoying themselves.'

'Yes. You are right.' Anna agreed with her after a moment's thought. 'It's to do with escape, isn't it? We all need that. I can quite see that.'

'Exactly! Escape – that's probably the right word too,' said Smiley good-naturedly. She found analysis tedious. She filled up their glasses again, hoping that Anna would talk about something else. She admired Anna with fervour. She was everything she could never be. Anna was intelligent, modest, feminine and wise – she knew who and what she was. Smiley had no clue about herself. She was unconventional and forever pursuing pleasure in the vain hope of finding this intangible thing she had always felt existed. Quite what, she had no idea – it had no name. But like a child who searches the rainbow's end in muddy fields, she constantly sought new things to excite her. Her attention span was short and she was rarely satisfied for long. She'd move on, restless, always searching but never finding this invisible thing. Her search made her promiscuous – her life unstructured – no aim – some would say quietly desperate. She lived for the day. But she was intelligent enough to know that she fooled herself. Other women did not like her. They thought she was dangerous. But few could match her extrovert warmth. Her honesty. Her straight-in-your-face opinions. She was gutsy and she was brave. Anna knew all this and loved her for it. She enjoyed her and just then, she felt curiously protected by her. Safe.

'Oh Anna – you are incredible. So self-effacing, so good. I'm not. I know I'm dreadful. Weak, superficial, fundamentally flawed.' In mock despair, she wailed, 'What shall I do? I wish I could be like you!'

'Rubbish!' retorted Anna with all the force of a volleyed tennis ball. 'To be me is to be little Miss Insignificant. Colourless and pathetic. You wouldn't last a day, Smiley. There are a thousand me's in the supermarkets; simply an epidemic of them. Going about their day in uneventful drabness and duty. Dressed like hell, uncombed with tired clean faces. You could never be that, my dear, sweet Smiley – but it's kind of you to say so anyway.' And the two women laughed together. The wine had reached their souls and released their thoughts. 'Me? I like the anonymity of my life. It's good to be invisible and go about my day with no one looking. It gives you a wonderful sort of freedom. No one actually caring, especially now of course.' Anna finished logically. There was no self-pity in her voice. She stared at her glass which she held before her with both hands hugged around it. 'I shall have to get used to that.'

'Oh 'Anna! He'll be back. He will.'

'Do you think so?' she asked quickly. 'There are precious few reasons to think that. It's so odd, Smiley, I have absolutely no idea where he is. For the first time in our married life. He could be in Russia for all I know. He's right off my radar screen.'

'Or in Argentina,' Smiley added silently. Anna picked up her thought.

'No. No, he's not gone after her, Smiley. I do know that. He's too defeated, too tired. Too damn married.'

Smiley could not bear the sudden heaviness that threatened to ruin their evening. It oppressed her. She wanted at all costs to avoid analysing the whole awful situation. 'Let's go out, Anna,' she said brightly. 'We'll have dinner in the little Italian place round the corner. It buzzes with life and it will do us both good.'

'That's a good idea. I'd love that.' Anna nodded her head. 'I'd like a quick bath first. And do you mind it I speak to Victoria before we go? I want her to do something for me.'

'Your counsellor?' Smiley teased her. 'Course. There's the telephone – help yourself.' She gave Anna a small hug. 'We all think you are fantastic,' she said simply. Then she turned and left the room.

Anna gazed at the carpet. Then looked out of the windows set high up on the wall. Lights twinkled against the dark London sky. She imagined the many other women who, like her, were on their own out there. It made her shiver. Was this what life without Johnny was like? Some women had the choice to be alone – others did not. She was one of the latter. The rest, like Smiley, never made the choice. Anna fell into a morbid trance. She traced possibilities for herself. A job. A course in computer literacy, alternative therapies perhaps. What on earth did a woman of her age do in order to hang on to her sanity? What could she offer anyone except fantastic fish pie, home made cakes, beautifully laundered sheets? She laughed out loud, bleakly. Perhaps she could teach people to drive, to garden, to paint. Was official occupation so imperative? Was it merely so she could hold her head up and say, 'Yes, that's me – I run the gardening course here – yes, in conjunction with the painting.' No! No! Anna sat up with a start as though she had been pinched. She straightened her back. She cleared her throat and stood up. She was horrified by the scenario she had conjured up for herself. With a shake of her head, she chased it away then she made her decision. She realised the risk. Her hand reached for the telephone. She dialled Victoria's number with hurried determination.

'Hello. It's Anna here. Could you organise something for me? Get a pen and jot this down.' Once done, she sat back and sighed deeply. For the first time in her life she had made a decision on her own – one that could change everything.

Victoria said nothing while she scribbled instructions on her pad. She simply confirmed that she understood and read them back. 'I'll see it's done tomorrow.' Inwardly she winced. Was there no end to Anna's accommodating nature – her magnanimity? Why did she always put herself out for others? Was this a form of service and did her Christian beliefs really teach her to exonerate others and overlook their blazing faults – some would say, sins? And for what? She should save herself first. But who could tell her this. Victoria's profession had taught her to be outwardly impartial unless asked. Anna was careful not to do this. Her call was short, precise and done with an attitude of new authority. In other words, I trust you but don't interfere.

It was Victoria's private opinion that the third world would have been a far worthier cause. This was one very dead horse – as far as she was legally, emotionally and intellectually concerned.

Smiley gave a little knock. 'Ready?' she asked. She peered round letting a lovely rush of scent come in with her.

'Absolutely,' replied Anna. 'Here I am – ready to hit London by night. How do I look?'

'You look great,' Smiley told her truthfully.

'Then that makes two of us,' said Anna. She was so slender, so delicately made. It took her new beautifully cut clothes to show her off and bring to life what she chose to hide. Like opening a drawer and finding some pretty ornament that had been put away years ago.

'I've booked a little table for us – 8 o'clock – so if we go now we can have a lovely drink first.'

'Another? I don't think I can.' The thought sickened her.

'Course you can.' Smiley took her arm. 'You can't weaken now. It's only just beginning, your new life.'

'Don't be ridiculous,' said Anna. 'I'll never let go of the old – you know that.'

Smiley heard her words and smiled back at her with undisguised admiration. 'Come on, Saint Anna – off we go,' she said. 'We've had a lovely day and I for one intend to celebrate it.'

The next morning Anna woke early with the instinctive urgency to go home. She did not for one moment consider what it would be like. She simply longed to hide in her house or in her garden. It would be far better than this. Another day in London would stifle her. She wanted more than anything else to be alone. She had to prepare herself for what was to come. Her strength had always come from solitude. She longed now for uncompromising silence. As the train took her west, she sat and gazed out of the window. Her newspaper lay unread before her. Her eyes flickered restlessly but took in everything along the route. She relaxed visibly as the cluttered urban mass gave way to the beautiful familiar downs. She felt a small smile cross beneath the surface of her face. Like a greeting – and a relief. Yes. This was home – whatever happened now, she'd never leave this part of England. She'd get through this bit of her life. She'd be all right.

Her mind was quite neutral as she drove home. Oddly peaceful, oddly calm. She thought of very ordinary things. Simple day-to-day things. Would the roses be out? How many eggs would she find in the run? Would Sixpence be there to meet her? She always was. She'd have to ring Mrs. Lane and ask her to walk Fudge back to her. Perhaps that could wait – she'd decide tomorrow. She'd go to the shop later. But then, what was being said? Her heart thumped a bit faster and in one second her unreal mood of calm changed. A little rush of panic swept all over her. Of course everyone must be talking – it was only natural. She abhorred the idea of being singled out for speculation. It made her want to run away. Be utterly invisible. Damn it! Why should she? She had done nothing wrong.

She pressed down further on the accelerator and drove up to the front of the house as though she was late. It stood before her untouched – the shutters firmly closed. A light breeze rustled through the creeper and gave it some life. The sun shone on the grey stone and lit away some of the gloom.

Anna sat and stared before her. The house could be a convent – just then so austere and still. It too meditated and wondered where its owners were. Their absence had been much longer than usual. Without people, it does not take long for a house to die.

With artificial energy, Anna flung open the car door. She kicked it with her foot quite forgetting her beautiful new shoe. She lugged four suitcases from the boot, dragging them over the gravel. She had left with only one. She opened the front door and stood in the darkened hall. Quickly she threw open the shutters; her steps resounding like little sharp echoes on the flagstones. She scooped up the post and went to the kitchen – silence – but for the old clock on the wall. She stood quite still for a moment – the tick-tock, normally so comforting, so wonderfully permanent – now sounded eerie. She moved then, rapidly to the garden. Sixpence saw her and fell from the apple tree. With brisk running steps the cat came towards her, meowing breathlessly. Anna picked her up and held her firmly. The warm furry body vibrated with purrs of ecstasy. The half-closed eyes announced utter bliss. The uncomplicated welcome comforted Anna. No words needed. No explanation either. She held Sixpence who was happy to be tucked beneath her arm ~~her~~ while she walked. Food would be at the end. Home.

Three days passed. Anna sat; she waited; and she waited. The telephone did not ring once. There was no crunch of car tyres on the gravel. She wanted to ring Yvonne but did not. What would she say? 'Have you heard from Mr. Carr?' or 'Is he there at the moment?' or 'When did you last see him?'
No. She could not bring herself to do it. To ask any of the questions would be to reveal too much. She'd lay herself wide open – to what? Pity? Ridicule?

Where was Johnny? Nothing else on earth mattered but an answer to that. If this silence went on much longer, Anna knew she'd have to get in touch with the police. Oh God! The very idea made ice hit her stomach. To register his disappearance in formal terms made her buckle.

What if he was dead? The thought had never once crossed her mind. Johnny dead – ABSURD! What a thought! But she remembered how he had looked only a few days ago. It now seemed like weeks. How had he looked? 'Finished!' she said out loud to the deaf four walls of the kitchen. 'Finished. That's how.' Anna got to her feet, feeling sick. She held her arms tightly against her stomach. Only tears came. Hot and gushing, they ran down her cheeks and splashed on the floor.

The telephone rang. The sound cracked through her like a shock – it made her jump. Hastily, she wiped her face as though she was about ~~the~~ to open the front door. She steadied herself and picked up the receiver. 'Hello.'

'Mrs. Carr?'

'Yes.'

'Hello, it's Yvonne here.'

Anna could think of nothing to say but, 'Yes.'

'I'm wondering if Mr. Carr is with you….'

'Not at the moment, Yvonne, I'm afraid. Perhaps I can help?'

Anna clung to the receiver, gripping it tightly. Her palms sweated.

'I need to speak to him urgently, Mrs. Carr. You see….'

'I'll get him to call when he comes in.' She did not say 'back'.

Like fraudsters, they conversed in pretence of normality. Like doctors with the terminally ill.

'Are you keeping well?' Yvonne's voice changed and was thick with the soft notes of kindness.

Anna's eyes welled again. She was feeble in the face of sympathy and just then would have welcomed Yvonne's company in her kitchen. Together they could have made a pot of tea and commiserated. Instead, she stiffened and said rather too briskly, 'Quite well, thank you, Yvonne. What about you? How is Lennie?'

'Oh we are fine, thank you. Always busy. Both of us.'

'Best way to be,' said Anna trying to sound buoyant.

'Well good-bye then.' Yvonne hung up. Silence. Followed by more silence. Anna came to understand the meaning of 'deafening silence'. Until then, she had found it a riddle. Now it was a physical reality.

Another day came and went. Waiting. Deafening silence.
'Be patient. He'll be back,' Victoria said,
'When?'
'Hard to say – but certainly within the fortnight.'
'Fortnight! You might just as well say three years. Each day feels like a life.'
Victoria nodded. She had seen all this before – many times. Nothing caused more subjective emotion and pain than domestic unrest. She knew it was wrong to be overly sympathetic. She'd not show Anna just how deeply she shared her dilemma, her anguish. To do so, would be to admit alarm, and that would not help anybody.

'Have you thought, Anna, how you will receive him? I mean, have you thought if you will be able to forgive him?' Anna did not answer her and Honor felt it would not be right to ask again. She herself was utterly disgusted with Johnny. She could not imagine how she was ever going to look him in the face again. The perfect husband! But of course, in the back of her mind was the growing disquiet that if it happened to Anna – could it not also happen to her? Why not?

Smiley said, 'Don't take him back, Anna. I've thought about it a lot. It's not worth the candle. You'll have to listen to all the crap about why and because etc., etc. And then when you've heard it all, you'll be expected NEVER to

mention it again – and to behave as though it never happened. And why the hell should you do that? Think about it – how will that make you feel?' Smiley shook her head. 'No. You must move on, be brave. Just move on.'
Again Anna said nothing. She just listened carefully to all the advice. She did not answer because quite simply she had no answers just then.

Beside her bed she had made a little calendar of fourteen squares. She crossed off one each morning before doing anything else. Today she had reached the eighth day of absence. It made her tremble. They had never been apart for this long.

Fragile. She ached all over. She forced herself out of bed as to stay there would be to sink. She'd never rise again. She threw a handful of coarse salt into her bath and ran a hot gushing tap over it. She yawned continually – the night had given her no respite. She vaguely thought she should see her doctor, but then again, it would mean interrogation. She chased the idea away. No doctor on earth could cure Hell. It would be over soon. Today even. Perhaps today would bring him back. She pulled her nightie off and with slow, careful movements, like the elderly, got into the hot water. Bliss. She sighed deeply and handed herself over to the enveloping heat. It comforted her.

Fudge pushed his way into her bedroom. He looked for her there. She heard him whining, unnaturally. He came in the bathroom, to the edge of the bath. She felt his breath on her shoulder. Once reassured of her presence, he sank with relief on to the mat. He tried to wag his tail but it was not the usual flourish. Anna saw he was in pain. Her wet hand touched his head and he looked at her with mournful eyes. 'What is it? What's wrong? Fudge, where's the pain?' He whined softly and tried to get up. He could not. The effort was too great and his back legs seemed to buckle. Anna frowned and the worry made her leave her bath, dress, and crouch down beside him. She talked gently all the time. He moved closer and constantly licked her hands. He did not get up. Anna decided to call the vet. Quickly she brought the telephone to where he lay. Her hand never left his head. 'I can't move him, I don't think. I'd rather not.'

'All right, Mrs. Carr. Leave him where he is and Mr. Davies will be with you in twenty minutes. I'm booking this as an emergency.'

'Whatever,' said Anna. 'Just get here.'

'You'll be all right, Fudge, don't worry. Mr. Davies is on his way.'

Too tired, she did not consider the reasons for Fudge's sudden decline.

'Johnny, Johnny, where are you?' she whispered.

Yvonne counted too.

'Today will be the day. I know it. Eight has always been my number, Lennie.'

Superstition and mild magic often offer hope and consolation in times of bewilderment. There are people who set their day by prophecy. The power is potent, the proof often beyond doubt, at least to the believer's interpretation.

'He'll ring today. I can feel it. Then I can tell him the good news. That will change everything.'

Lennie said that he hoped so, but he could not help but wonder how Mrs. Carr was going to recover from all this.

Yvonne was right. At 11.30 Mr. Carr rang her. Cheerful, steady, the same. Stunningly oblivious to the worry his absence had caused. Relief put anger to one side. She cleared her throat with a small nervous cough.

'Mr. Carr, we have some wonderful news for you.'

'Oh really? And what could that possibly be, Yvonne?' His voice now quite different; flat and tired.

'We have a mystery buyer – and they have already put a lot of money in the account.'

Silence – She could hear him breathe. And then,

'How - how much? What do you mean by a lot?'

'Three hundred thousand pounds – no less.' Loyal triumph laced her voice.

'Good Heavens! Are you quite sure? Who has done this?' His voice was sceptical, tinged with sarcasm. Yvonne must have got it wrong. He refrained from telling her to have her eyes tested.

'Positive. Really Mr. Carr. I CAN read a bank statement you know. Come and see for yourself.'

'No letter, Yvonne? There must be something.'

'Yes. A short note to say an order would follow. But that's all.' On saying it out loud, it did seem unreal to her, she had to admit.

'It's ludicrous, Yvonne. No one behaves like that.' And he laughed curtly.

'It has to be some awful joke, I'm afraid. Who do we know who hates us so much to do this?' He thought then said, 'It's bloody unkind.'

But Yvonne remained resolute. 'It's not a joke – I've checked it over and over again. The money is genuine – it's yours.' She let him absorb this, then said, 'Come back, Mr. Carr, come and see for yourself. We are all waiting for you to return.' He did not reply. 'Mr. Carr? You are still there?'

'I am,' he answered punctually. 'Yvonne?'

'Yes – and I'm here too,' she told him. A smile on her face.

'Yvonne. What must you all think of me? I've been such a fool.'

'Well, we all think you are a bloody good bloke and that's the truth.'

He sent a gusty laugh straight into her ear. It was a good sound. 'I've missed you,' she told him simply. 'And the lads don't know what is going on. They miss you too.'

'I'll be in tomorrow.'

'Now, is that a promise – or do I still have to worry?'

'It's a promise,' Johnny paused. 'Er – Yvonne – do you happen to have news of Mrs. Carr? I've tried to ring but…'

'She's well. At least she appeared to be when we spoke. Mrs. Carr is always the same, no matter what.'

Johnny's throat swelled and he could not answer her just then. He put the receiver down.

Home. But home to what?

It is women who tempt – it is men who are tempted.
This is a fact – it is basic biology.
It is women who forgive – it is men who are forgiven.
It is women who are powerful – it is men who are powerless – the shorn Samsons.
It is women who save – it is men who are saved.
But it is man who leads as the lover – and it is woman who receives him and is enfolded by him.
It is men who love more deeply – it is women who take their hearts and do what they will.
It is women who are clever – it is men who are not.
With brimming ardour and restless loins, they allow themselves to be used.
A man's heart, once given, becomes a steady, vulnerable vessel – it is easily shattered in the hands of the user.
Temptation has nothing to do with love.

Johnny had not been able to see beyond Sol's creamy, olive skin – the mesmeric red of her mouth. Physically, he had been overwhelmed, his own self obliterated by the intensity of temptation. Who could ever have warned him of that? Who could have put a hand on his shoulder and stopped him? And would he have listened? No. Not then. How could he when he was not master of himself?

And now, with petrifying midday clarity, he was running home. Guilty. Confused. He now longed for the utter familiarity of his wife. The uncomplicated purity of everything that was her.

What if she had discovered everything? No – no – that was not possible. How could she? There was simply no connecting way that she could. He discarded the thought with complete confidence. A small surge of strength reached through him. He had something to tell her, something of substance. He came home bearing gifts. The money! Never mind the origin. Once Anna knew they were safe, life could begin again. She would forgive him for having walked away, for having been so callous to her, the person he most loved in the whole wide world. She need never know the rest.

Johnny drove for hours. Along the narrow country lanes, he took no particular direction. But he kept within a certain radius of home, and Anna.

What would she be doing when he arrived? He tried to imagine how she would look. Her sweet face – her hair. He'd take her away. Anywhere she wanted to go – Venice perhaps? They had often spoken of that. He'd buy her some lovely clothes – a new bag. Anything she wanted. A ring. A ring to commemorate. His guilt would go with time and the resumption of their life. The wonderful cosy order restored. This fractured episode would fade. Johnny prayed as he drove – 'Please let it be alright.'

Fudge died with his head on Anna's lap, the vet talking quietly while he administered the injection. She did not cry, bravely, she watched everything. The kind strong hands that controlled life's transition into death. The supreme care he took, words softly spoken but with masculine firmness. The deep tones of that voice seemed to contain a knowledge and authority that gave the moment a harrowing peace. And while Anna watched, she planned where she'd dig the grave in the orchard. She wanted to bury him before he was cold. She could not bear the thought of him being cold.

'I'll help you,' Mr. Davies told her. 'We'll do it right away. I've plenty of time.'

'How very kind,' she managed to say. Deeply touched by any sympathy, Anna's eyes brimmed with tears. She really did not care just then to hide what she felt. The vet had heard rumours and realised her grief was more than this. She was far too thin. 'I'll fetch a spade,' she told him.
Gently and with angelic respect, she lifted Fudge's head from her lap. She extricated herself and with soft steps, left the room. Mr. Davies followed when he knew she was gone. He lifted Fudge and carried him downstairs. An everyday event for him, but today, he was curiously moved. There was something pitifully alone about Mrs. Carr. She was a fine lady. He'd stay until he saw she was alright. Together and in gloomy silence, they dug a hole beneath the apple tree where Fudge had often sat.

'Wait!' Anna suddenly ran into the house and brought back an old overcoat. 'My husband's,' she said simply and kneeling down, she placed it at the bottom of the grave. Then between them they lowered Fudge down. Anna folded the coat over him. Softly she said, 'Goodbye.' She watched as the vet threw earth on him. Watched him scoop and cup soil in both hands and sprinkle it over the lifeless dog. His hands were large, kind and strong. She did not blink until the body was obscured and taken from her forever. Once done, Mr. Davies offered Anna his arm and pulled her to her feet. He held her firmly and did not release her until certain she was steady.

'Thank you.' she said. They stood for a moment looking down on the rich brown mound of earth – the chilly evidence of death. Sixpence lay above them in the tree. She mewed loudly. Anna raised her arms and the cat came down to her swiftly.

'Let's have that drink now.' And they walked to the kitchen. There they spoke of local things; his work, her garden. Safe solid things. Mr. Davies was careful to keep the conversation neutral. He finished his drink and smiled kindly. Despite the occasion, he had enjoyed himself. It had been a privilege to help her. She was a lady of courage and grace. She inspired respect; and the desire to protect her. He smiled at his thoughts as he drove slowly back to the practice. Professional perspective soon banished romantic thoughts – pigs were his next appointment.

Anna took her drink back to the apple tree. She slumped against it and let her tears fall fast and thick down her face. A bad day - a day of relentless sadness. She knew she had reached her limits. On unsteady feet, she returned to the kitchen and poured out another drink. Much stronger now she was alone. To hell with the lady-like measure. She threw back her head and let the vodka slide down. The taste disgusted her, the effect did not. She began to feel a hilarity take hold of her. It threatened to take her either way, laughing or screaming and out of control.

'Hello.' Quietly behind her. And there he stood. Her unfaithful husband. Her husband of twenty-eight years. He looked the same. Healthy. Fit. He smiled at her. His smile was cautious and on closer observation, his eyes were bloodshot and strained.

She flew at him.

And before either could think, she struck him with staggering force across his left cheek. The swing of her arm gave her hand extra clout and she saw she had hurt him. She was thrilled to see it.

'Bastard!' She spat at him. 'You bastard.'

He tried to catch her wrist but she evaded him. She reached for a mug on the table and she hurled it at his head. It missed. Helplessly, she looked about for something else, but there was nothing to hand. Johnny stepped towards her and grabbed both her arms. He pinned them to her sides and pulled her towards him. Much stronger than her, he had no difficulty in restraining her. He noticed how thin she was.

'Hello,' he said again, looking into her face. She looked wild. No, not wild – deranged. She struggled like a netted hare and when she could, she punched out at him. He could feel her fury and her pain. She was wretched and she looked wretched, without him, she had diminished.

'I'm drunk,' she told him. 'Can't you tell?'

'You are drunk – but does it have to make you so violent? Most people become happier when they drink.'

'Really? Not me, why should I?' She said. 'There is absolutely nothing to be happy about. Nothing to celebrate, unless of course, you can think of something?'

Johnny searched her face. 'Oh but there is,' he told her quietly. But was she ready to hear? He assessed her mind – the patterns it was bringing up. He had never seen his wife like this. Her misery stood naked between them like some heavy dark portrait that displays the bleeding heart. Johnny's remorse threatened to stumble him. Quickly, he told himself that he had returned bringing hope. Their future safe and grassy-pathed. He held a torch in his hand.

'Anna, all is well. We are going to be all right. ' Pause. Let her take it in. 'We have a new order. We have a lot of money now.'

She heard the words and for her the moment was a crossroads. Her anger was so great that she was consumed and surprised with her own feelings. Slowly she turned and looked at this man. And she wondered. . .

Did she really want him back?

Did she honestly need him?

Why?

Her husband's crumpled face. Her husband's unfaithful body. Too recent. Too raw.

'What is wrong, Anna?' she heard him say.

'What is wrong?' she echoed. 'Don't you mean what is right?'

He tried to get closer to her, but she stepped back.

'You are tired, Anna. Let's go and sit in the garden. We need to get used to one another again.'

'Yes.' She looked directly at him then. 'You are right. I am tired. As a matter of fact, I've never been so bloody tired.' Flat voice. Dead face.

'Well, come on.' He held out his hand. 'Let's go to the rose garden.'

He spoke gently to her well aware of the dangerous axis they were on. But to lose her now! It would make him desperate. He knew he would never be able to cope. She did not take his hand but she allowed him to put an arm on her thin shoulder. He guided her out to the garden. Together they sat on the wooden seat in silence. The garden watched them, the air heavy with anticipation. Life tiptoed around them – waiting. The decision was Anna's.

'You are tired,' he said again. Tender. He rubbed her shoulders with slow rhythmic movements that lulled her. Human touch, hand on skin – a healing, calming force. She shut her exhausted eyes and felt the perimeters of safety rise up around her. That one hand was the only thing she felt in her life then. Her body gave a little shudder. Silently he planned. Both fragile. Both vulnerable to terminal fracture. He'd need all his skill to get through this.

Anna's head fell against him. He caught her to him and held her – she slept. Her face had left the day. He carried her, feather-light, to their room. He laid her down with all the gentle care of a father. He covered her and kissed her forehead. Then he stepped back and found the old chair nearby. He sat down and waited for her. His anxiety immobilised him. Two hours.

It was dark when she woke. The day had vanished and she wondered if she had dreamt of Johnny's return. She lay in bed in her day clothes – she had no idea how long she had been there. She dreaded being awake, but somewhere she heard, 'Here I am! Over here.'
She sat up and saw the outline of his head against the window. He sat in the old chair.

'Johnny!' she called. Her voice unnaturally loud. 'It is you, isn't it?'
He laughed softly and came over to her. 'It is,' he said. She moved to make a place for him to sit. Immediately she blurted,

'There is something I must tell you.' Her tone urgent. He stroked back her hair. He touched her face with the back of his hand.

'And what could that be?' he asked, carefully.
She straightened her back and braced herself. 'Fudge is dead, Johnny. He died today.' She paused to look at him. She knew it would upset him. Already she cushioned him. 'I've buried him under his favourite tree. You know the one.' He nodded, his eyes never leaving her face.

'All by yourself?'

'No. With kind Mr. Davies' help. He was quite wonderful and looked after us all. He can put me down any time he likes!'

Johnny put his arms around her then. He breathed in the smell of her hair. 'You are a brave girl,' he said. 'It must have been horrible and very sad.'

'It was. But I wrapped him in your old coat to keep him warm and comfortable. I couldn't bear the. . .' Anna did not want to think about it just then. It was just too much – too tired to cry anymore.

'Poor old chap. We shall miss him,' Johnny stated simply. At this moment he could not focus on Fudge either.

'We will,' she said.

He stroked her hair, slowly, thoughtfully. Neither spoke. After a while, he sat her back against the pillows – and he smiled at her. 'Are you hungry?' he asked. 'Let's go downstairs and have something to eat. I'll go and get it ready.'

He left her then and she got up. She washed her face, splashing it with cold water. She felt better, brighter. Happier. The face she saw in the mirror told her as much. It had regained some of its colour. She pinched her cheeks and saw deep rose suffuse her skin. She went on staring at herself like an onlooker. She saw the face smile – a rather small secret smile. She saw light in its eyes. As in a trance and standing very still, she heard her own voice then. It was low but certain.

'Human fallibility,' said her voice. She listened attentively. And again. 'Human fallibility.'

Now the face she watched smiled more openly. She felt a change come over her – an optimistic breeze. Life gave a little hum, a halo of hope.

Downstairs classical music filled the kitchen – wonderful vibrant notes – the cello above all else. Its swollen bursting sounds pitched up to Anna's room and she imagined Johnny beneath her, preparing their dinner and their future. The softer notes of the piano now took over from the frenzied cello and below, Johnny was enfolded by the utter beauty of it. He moved, dreamlike about the kitchen. He found various things that could be put together for their dinner. But no champagne. Instead a bottle of white wine that had been standing in the fridge for weeks. That would have to do. As he beat the eggs, the cello returned with rousing gusto. Johnny paused to turn up the music. He began to feel wonderfully happy.

Immersed in what he did and what lay ahead, he did not hear the front door open. Nor did he hear the steps in the hall; on the staircase moving swiftly. They slowed on reaching the top and lost confidence on reaching Anna's door. Apprehensive like a school boy outside the headmaster's door. Silence. The intruder listened, irritated that his breathing caused the cellophane around the flowers he held, to crackle. With something that amounted to thrilling anticipation, his fist knocked softly on her door. He stepped back then and waited for the curtain to go up. The steps behind the door were quick-paced and muffled, the sound of which made his heart beat even faster. The door flew open and with it came the rush of flowery scent.

'Mr. Davies!' Anna opened the door wider. 'What are you doing here?' She smiled at him; that lovely gracious smile that held no secrets. Open and beautiful with all the honesty of a firm handshake. 'Have you left something behind? It's awfully late. You should have rung instead and I would have dropped it off...' But then she saw the flowers. The vibrant yellow of a dozen sunflowers. She could smell the honey that came from them. Deep within her mind and no longer buried by the cluttered present, she recalled with shocking immediacy the fields of them that had so intoxicated her young eyes. Her paints, her senses.

'They are for you; for you and Fudge. I thought you could put them on his grave.'
She stared at him then, touched beyond words. She was not sure what to do next. It had been years since anyone had given her flowers. To her they symbolised much more, so much more than a mere gift. Flowers came with feelings, secret messages. Unspoken words. Especially these. How could he have known? She held out her hands and took them from him. She held them to her making them her very own. A honeyed bunch of bright sunshine. Juan. The girls. Maria. Anna felt a swell of emotion reach over her. Mr. Davies watched as she bit her lower lip.
'Thank you. It is quite the kindest thing anyone has ever done for me.' She bent her head and buried her face in the profusion of petals and smell. He watched, pleased that what had taken courage to do turned out to be so well received.

'It's not much. You deserve so much more...' The tone of his voice made her look up at him.

'Do I?' she asked with her usual daytime candour. He smiled. His healthy outdoor face luminous with admiration.

'I think so. I've never met such a brave lady.' And she felt the kindness radiate from his hazel eyes – strong, wholesome, wise. Her own studied him carefully. Above the flowers she watched him.

Finally she said, 'You cannot imagine what sunflowers mean to me – you cannot have guessed, surely?'

He smiled back at her. 'Just a lucky choice – I know your garden is full of roses!'

'Well – thank you. Thank you.' She paused aware that he looked at her intently. Aware too of a certain awkwardness; the vet standing outside her bedroom door. Eight thirty at night. Bringing her a bunch of flowers!

'I'm dressing for dinner, Mr. Davies – I'm so sorry not to be able to offer ....' He did not listen to more. He stepped towards her and before Anna could move, he kissed her. Incredible soft tenderness filled her mouth. She tasted peppermint and felt the unfamiliar ripples of response. It swept gently through her but did not overtake her. It was wildly pleasant – unthreatening. A channel of goodness brought to her from a solid country heart. It did not seek to control or take her away. Anna dropped her flowers. Her arms reached up and she held him to her. Dazed and breathless, she pulled away. He did not try to get her back. But with extraordinary reverence in his voice he said,

'You're beautiful.' His eyes now lit with a certain triumph. He stooped down and picked up her flowers. He handed them to her. 'For you and Fudge – for your bravery these last weeks.'

'Oh!' Anna gave a little gasp. So he knew! Did that mean he felt sorry for her? Was that what all this was about? His face told her otherwise. She smiled at him aware for one split second of equality – no one else involved. Sacred. Their unique secret. No one and nothing could ever take it away. It made them feel good and inwardly radiant. 'You must go now – please.'
He nodded and understood. For as they stood now in silence, they heard the music below. It seemed to fill the hall. Mr. Davies turned and was gone. He did not look back and Anna stood on the landing watching, mesmerised, as he disappeared through the front door. Like some giddy girl she touched her mouth with her free hand. Her tongue ran along her top lip. Yes. It was peppermint. Still there. Delivered so gently to her. Along with the honey and the yellow. She returned to her room and lay the flowers on her bed. She filled a waste paper bin with water and placed them in it. Then she opened one of her cupboards and pushed them right to the back, in darkness, for the night. It was the most devious thing she had ever done throughout her married life. And of course the kissing!
Human fallibility! Anna smiled back at herself in the mirror. Her face was pink in acknowledgement to Mr. Davies.
She turned away and walked with quick steps. She went to her cupboard. It bulged with new clothes. She ran her hands along the rail, lifting out two hangers. She chose her

clothes very carefully. She laid them on her bed – fetched her Italian shoes. And then with meticulous attention, she dressed for dinner.

'Good heavens! You look . . . You look absolutely beautiful.' Johnny could not believe his eyes. 'Is this my wife?'

Anna walked towards him, her thin legs as elegant as a greyhound, her body chic and girlish. Her Italian clothes understatedly sexy. She had painted her face pale rose, her hair well brushed and full.

'My God!' Johnny put down the wooden spoon and met her. She invited him, he read that. Her face turned up to his. He kissed her. He kissed her like he had not kissed her for many years. And he went on kissing her – and she responded like she had not done for many years. Their feelings, like familiar strangers fused like jacks-in-the box, finally unlidded. Long overdue.

They did not eat that night after all. They did not emerge from their room until much later the following day. Between love, they talked in murmured voices. Anna played with him and he, now assured that all was well, played back. He told her repeatedly how much he loved her.

This is a declaration said countless times all over the world, but each time it is unique.

She told him how rich he was.

'Where did the money come from?'

'I have no idea yet. But we will know soon.' He was genuinely puzzled. Anna smiled in the dark. And then her mouth was against his,

'Perhaps you can afford to buy me a car now,' she said. 'Anything I like.'

'Maybe,' he said sleepily. 'But let's go to Venice first.'

'When?' She was wide awake and wanted to go on playing all night. She lifted her head. 'When?' she whispered playfully. But her husband slept. She knew he felt safe now that he had got her back. Order restored. Johnny had always hated disruption. Anna lay on her back. She could feel her life slipping back into familiar boundaries, ones she understood. To venture outside them was to enter the bull ring without the sword, the cape. She closed her eyes in gratitude. To what? To whom? To the peace she now felt. To the wonderful velvet cloak of security that now enfolded her. She turned over on her side and felt a private bliss. It seemed to settle all about her. There was honey in the air – and hidden vibrant yellows. Their room was filled with all good things. Like waving flags. Happy children. A second chance. Anna drifted into sleep, sedated by Johnny's return, by his love. Dazed by Mr. Davies' kindness. She could not think about it properly then. She knew it was good, brought on wings of generosity that did not expect a reply. The truest form of esteem in an ideal world.

And then lastly, she thought of Juan. Her eyes flickered open then. She looked into his face and he smiled back at her.

'Ridiculous girl!' he said. She imagined how he'd laugh if she told him Mr. Davies had told her she was beautiful.

'Are you sure, Anna? Quite certain of that? There must be some mistake.'

Her thoughts drifted slowly from her and into her pillow. With her arm on Johnny's shoulder she let her lids close and take her into night.

'I've tried all day, Lennie, to get through to them. There's no reply.'

Lennie smiled and winked,

'Thank God for that' he said.

'Huh! So she never confronted him – is that it? He has got away with it, hasn't he? Completely. I can't believe it.' Smiley snorted in disgust.

'Well, yes, I suppose he has,' said Victoria. 'Anna obviously thought it better to deal with it like that – and leave it all behind.'

'She's a saint – we all know that.' Stated Honor with undisguised admiration.

'I'm sure Johnny realises just how lucky he is.'

'Really?' said Smiley scornfully. She raised one eyebrow.

'If you ask me, he needs a bloody good thrashing. Have we already forgotten the hell he put Anna through? No man should be allowed to get away with that.'

'Why are you so cross?' Victoria asked her. 'Surely you know that is happens every day – to countless women. This is no different, believe me, Smiley.'

Honor said, 'She has stuck to her vows – I knew she would.' Her face was lit with quiet approval. 'Anna would never let anything stand in the way of her love for Johnny.'

'Hm.' Victoria was thoughtful. 'I think that Anna has done exactly what suits her. Johnny will never leave her again – he never meant to in the first place. We can all be pretty sure of that.' Honor nodded in fervent agreement, adding,

'He adores her too. How could he not?'
The three women sat in silence, united by the realisation that Anna now held all the cards. She was unknowingly powerful.

'Well.' said Smiley after a while. 'I still think she should have confronted him. It's ridiculous to behave as though she knew nothing. I don't like the thought of her being made a fool of – not Anna.'

'A fool! That's the last thing she is, Smiley. Anna is wise – smarter than any of us. That's how she's coped with the whole damn business. She knows absolutely what she is doing. We must all of us respect that, and of course, the outcome.' With this, Victoria considered the case closed.

'Quite.' acknowledged Honor. She stared at the table, visibly troubled.

'You are suddenly very pale, Honor – what's wrong?' Smiley scanned her face with genuine concern. Victoria did the same. She managed to say quite kindly,

'Yes – you are. It's not 'flu I hope?'

'I'm alright,' she told them in a small voice.

'Most unconvincing.' Victoria told her with her usual directness.

'But you're not, Honor.' Smiley used a much softer tone.

'Well if I'm not, it's not my fault.' She said, her words spilling out from a trembling mouth. Her face had become even whiter. Hastily, she began to pick up her things to go. Victoria grabbed her gloves.

'Oh no you don't,' she said. 'Come on, you are not going anywhere until you have told us what is wrong with you.' She patted Honor's arm. 'We are your friends, you know.'

Honor acknowledged this with a weak smile. She dreaded talking about herself. She was so reserved and had always preferred the background. It took immense courage for her to say, 'It's Gerald. I think he's having an affair.' She cupped her chin in her hand in order to control the facial shivers this announcement caused.

Stunned, Smiley blurted, 'Honor – you can't be serious!' Her voice full of scorn. 'Who on earth with?' Her tone insulting as it implied impossibility. Quickly she rectified her blunder and said, 'I'm sorry, Honor – I didn't mean it like that.'

Victoria kicked her under the table and gave her a meaningful look. It said, 'You and I may think he is a nightmare but she does not. He is her life.'

'What a fucking bastard.' Smiley could think of nothing else to say just then. 'Are you absolutely certain, Honor?'

'Pretty much so,' she replied, choosing to ignore the bad language. 'He's walking differently.'

'How so?' Victoria cocked her professional head. She felt dreadfully sorry for her.

'More lively. You know, there's more spring in his step. Lots of little signs – I know him so well. I can tell.'

Honor would not be able to cope with this. She was not womanly. She would not be clever with Gerald. She was just too doormat nice and of course, she'd mope. This would only aggravate matters.

But Gerald for heaven's sake! It would take a brave woman. Or a desperate one. Who on earth would want to find an enormous cod on the pillow in the morning; and that gaping mouth! Victoria shuddered inwardly. Smiley's disgust was more apparent.

'Since when?' they asked together.

'Since a month ago, perhaps a little longer. I can't be sure. She's young, you see – about thirty I think.'

Then you are a dead dog, thought Smiley. Who was going to tell Honor this? 'You must speak to Anna, she will tell you what to do.'

Honor smiled limply. 'I will,' she said. Then she sat up very straight, 'I shan't let him go, you know – never. He is my life – and I am his.' Her lips were stubbornly pursed together. Smiley looked up at the ceiling. This simplistic assumption irritated her. Didn't Honor know that in this sort of game two plus two very rarely made four. Hadn't life taught her anything?

'It's sex; you do realise that, don't you?' Smiley blurted out again.

'Quite. I know that.' Honor agreed in a very matter-of-fact voice. 'She provides what I can't. She feeds his ego. I stopped doing that a long time ago.' She stood up. 'I only provide food. And now I must go. Today is Thursday and

Gerald likes fish.' She picked up her bag. 'I'll see you both next week – in here?' She surveyed them tiredly.

'Of course,' they both said together. They suddenly felt helpless to advise her. She was pitifully self-contained – her demeanour already one of burden and sacrifice. They watched her walk away.

'She's a poor devil, isn't she?' Smiley was the first to speak.

Victoria stared at the door through which Honor had disappeared. She nodded, agreeing with this opinion. 'Perhaps we all are one way or another,' she said thoughtfully. They sat in shared silence. They were both aware that Honor did not inspire strong feelings in either of them. It made them feel mildly uncomfortable. There was no fire about her secret, no edge to her dilemma. They would not reach for their spears to protect her. But of course, they would 'be there' for her – to catch her when she fell. A box of tissues. Of course they would. They had known her all their lives. 'I think she should see a councillor – both of them actually,' said Victoria. 'I'm sure that could be a great help.'

Smiley shook her head and paused in the act of lighting a cigarette. 'Bollocks, Victoria,' she said. 'Honour should buy some lipstick.'

Victoria's face lit up with amusement. She raised an eyebrow and said wickedly, 'Plus a little H.R.T?' Both women dissolved into laughter. They felt faintly disloyal at doing so and tried to stop. But it was useless.

'That wouldn't stand for "His Raging Tool", by any chance, would it?' asked Smiley. 'If so, I'm in total agreement.'

She had the last word.

The End
Of "Siesta"

PTO for:

The Prologue to
"The Man Who Danced with a Pig"

Part 2 of
The V.A.S.H. Quartet.

The Man Who Danced with a Pig
(Concerning Honor)

The Prologue

The decision to end her marriage was taken out of Honor's hands.

Callously Gerald told her, 'That's it, my dear. Our union is over.'

She had gasped. She could not think of anything appropriate to say. Eventually her face said it for her and crumpled into tears she could not stop. Through stinging eyes she looked at her husband and saw how much her show of distress irritated him. He was ready to bolt - that was clear. Between her whimpering sobs, she heard him say, 'You will have all the money you need and of course you must remain in this house.'

She watched as he looked about the tidy drawing - room; his eyes fixed briefly on the hunting pictures. She knew he rather loved those. The pale afternoon light enveloped the room enhancing the home counties affluence and the shared accumulation of precious things - and a thirty year marriage.

Gerald looked out beyond the French windows. His fleshy lips puckered together, while he allowed her time to take in all he had said and what it meant. Icy fear poured slowly over her brain and trickled into her heart which began to beat unnaturally fast. She squeezed her elbow against her ribs. Humiliation enveloped her. Her mind darted in all directions like some hysterical marlin caught on a vicious hook. What would she do without him? What would people say about her; about them? How on earth did a woman of her age manage? It was too dreadful to think about. Life without Gerald! Appalling. How could he do this to her? 'Why?' she heard a voice say, 'Why?'

Her husband moved uneasily in the arm chair not far from her. 'I simply think we've run our course, my dear. I need to be alone. People at our stage of life often do you know. Something to do with our mortality I think.' He attempted a little laugh.

'What about mine?' she asked. Her vulnerability made him wince. He did not want to be responsible for her. Her reliance unnerved him. It did not make him feel masterful anymore. He refused to acknowledge that it was he who had made her submissive. In the early days it had thrilled him - his dominance - his power over her.

Now she burdened him with her sexless servitude and plainness. He wanted something more exciting, Cruelly he compared her to Gillie. Even the way they breathed! Honor did not stand a chance.

Suddenly she got to her feet. She took two steps towards him and summoning up all her broken strength she managed to say, 'I hate you. You are horrible and selfish.'

Her school girl outburst displayed an innocence and lack of guile that assured her husband of victory. A raw vulnerability cultivated by a union of control and spineless servitude. She finished with, 'and I believe you to be a liar.' She did not wait for a reply. To his mild surprise, she turned and left the room. She had never spoken to anyone like that in her entire life.

Gerald now sat alone. He tapped the table beside him, as people did in waiting rooms. There was a smirk on his face. Well, that was not too difficult, he thought. He knew that once the blow had been delivered she would not put up much of a fight. He heard the car starting up. He got to his feet and walked towards the window. Hiding behind the curtain, he caught a glimpse of her hand as she pressed the button to open the electric gates. Then she was gone!
How many marriages ended this way - the car symbolic of rupture? He walked quickly to the telephone. He deliberated. Should he ring their son? No, he'd still be in his office. His hand picked up the receiver but as he did so, he was suddenly aware that he did not feel elated. A sea mist engulfed his resolve. Dampened his mind. The envisioned joy did not enfold him or congratulate his neat performance.
He replaced the receiver and put his hand deep into his pocket. The triumph had left his face and he now looked lost and foolish. His features flabby and collapsed. 'I'll ring Gillie later,' he told himself. 'I'll tell her the good news once the dust has settled.'

He felt a frisson of fear throb in the area of his throat and the reality of losing his large redbricked house and its immaculate two acres harpooned his entire being. Quickly he sought the restoration of order - the denial of change to come. He almost ran out of the French windows and regained authority by calling the gardener. 'Pete! Pete! Are you about?'

'Here I am, Mr. Bailey.' Gerald saw him spring to attention in the herbaceous border, a handful of weeds in his right hand.

'Ah! There you are! Could you stop doing that - and mow the lawn. Now.' Gerald was pleased that his voice sounded so steady. He always loved giving orders.

'But it was only done two days ago, Mr. Bailey. You can still see the stripes.'

'Now! I said. Do you hear me?' Gerald turned and disappeared into the house.

He did not hear Pete say, 'Silly old fool! His missus is worth ten of him!'

....

Honor drove in paralysed misery. Numb and unable to think properly, her sub-conscious protected her and she was aware that she had parked in front of a small and ugly hotel. It was now dark. She had to get out, go in and ask for a room. For how long? A week? A year? She got out of her car and stood on shaky legs. With sudden resolve she braced herself and walked through the door into a dark brown world that symbolised her own.

'Anyone about?' She heard herself call. 'I need a room.' She could smell old fried food and stale beer. Then welcome steps revealed a middle-aged man with a vast stomach and a happy face.

'Well my dear, what can we do for you this evening?' His smile was kind - his manner reassuring.

'I need a room please. With a bathroom if that's possible.' Should she say she was on her way somewhere? Explain herself?

'Certainly, my dear. Our rooms are all vacant and they are all en-suite.' He looked up at her. 'You look a little tired to me (his familiarity did not offend her) - so tonight we'll put you in Peg's room.'

'Peg's room?' Honor frowned.

'Its deluxe - our best. Now where is your bag?' She indicated her car, aware that she felt dizzy and sick. And hungry.

'I need to eat,' she told him weakly. 'Can something be sent to my room.?'

'Course. There'll be cut sandwiches done in a jiffy.'

'You are very kind - thank you.'

A few minutes later Honor lay back on a mauve counterpane, and from tired eyes surveyed the flowered wallpaper and the printed carpet. She inhaled the artificial smell of woodland flowers - the distant smell of cigarettes. She saw a tray with two cups and a kettle. And questioned whether she had the strength to make herself some tea. The distance from her bed to the tray seemed chasmic; but she got there. She'd remember that cup of tea for the rest of her life. And the sandwiches. Strong black tea drunk without milk - white bread sandwiches thick with salad cream and spam. Just then these things filled her world - were her world. She was like an abandoned animal that had found shelter and food. Suddenly she felt a little better - a return of energy – a warmth that fortified her. She had no idea what this meant. She washed the cup and put it back on the tray. Then she swept any crumbs she could see into the bin. Assured of order she turned and unpacked her nightdress. She washed her face, brushed her hair then pulled back the bedcovers. She lay on her back and closed her eyes. The moment she did this, the image of a wall appeared before her. It reached up into the sky. It was insurmountable. Panic flipped her eyes open and the wall disappeared. She clenched her fists and tried again. At last, sleep rescued her and oblivion brought a close to a day that marked the end of her married life.

Honor spent a week at the hotel - then returned to a silent house. She had no idea where Gerald was. He communicated with her through some lawyer. She saw no one for two months except her son, David. He told her to get on with it – get Gerald out of her life as quickly as possible. To keep herself busy. Doing what? She asked him. Anything, he'd said. Then . . . 'I can see you dancing, Mum.'

'Dancing? What do you mean?' Honor laughed at her son. He was being ridiculous; but kind.

'I mean it, Mum. I know you'd be good. You've always held yourself so well - I bet there's rhythm in those legs....'

'Oh stop it, David! You don't have to be so good to me . . .'

'I'm not! I'm just telling you what I think. Go on, give it a go!'

'And make a complete fool of myself?' Her son nodded.

'Yup,' he said. 'And make a complete fool of yourself!' He came over to her and put his arms around her. He hugged her tightly to him for one brief moment. 'Must get back now, Mum. Susie is waiting for me. Will you be okay?'

'Course!' she volleyed back, without thinking.

He picked up his brief case and walked towards the front door. 'Remember what I've said won't you?' And he gave a small wave. He was so like her in looks, with his auburn hair and pale skin. A face, that when animated, made people stare, attracted by a certain reassuring integrity. A much underestimated niceness inherited from his mother.

Honor's three friends sat around Anna's kitchen table and discussed her situation.

'What on earth will she do now?' asked Smiley. She was incredulous.

'Only God is qualified to answer that question.' Victoria was exasperated.

'If only she had taken our advice,' Smiley implored.

'What advice?' snapped Victoria. 'Are you mad? We never actually gave her any did we?' She paused. 'Oh yes - I do remember something but wasn't it very unsuitable anyway?' She rummaged in her bag for cigarettes. 'Too late now.'

Anna listened quietly. 'You need not worry about her you know. She stayed with us last night.'

'Oh?' Two faces turned to her - one kinder than the other.

'Yes. She's going to be absolutely fine. She has a new passion in her life. It's all she can talk about.'

'Really? And what might that be?' Victoria said behind clouds of smoke which she fanned with her newspaper.

'What's his name?' asked Smiley cheerfully.

'No, no! Not a man.' Anna shook her head.

'I didn't imagine it would be,' said Victoria drily.

'Nor I,' said Smiley philosophically. 'Not Honor. So it has to be a charity. Which one?'

'You're quite wrong,' Anna laughed at them both. 'Honor has taken up – the tango! She spends every single free hour she has learning to dance.'

'What?' gasped Victoria. 'It cannot be true. The tango is . . . is . . . ' She searched for words, 'is so wild - so sexy! Honor couldn't possibly do that. I simply don't believe it!'

'Well,' Anna beamed, 'that's what she is doing and she says it has changed her life. You don't always need a man to do that you know!'

Smiley's nod said, 'hear, hear.' Then she raised her glass and said, 'Well good for her. To Honor then and may she lose all honour soon.'

The women smiled in approval. Even Victoria now conceded the possibility, she certainly gave it her support.

'The waltz - yes - I can imagine that. But the tango? I just hope . . . ' She shrugged in still lingering doubt, then gave a conciliatory nod. 'I just hope they don't laugh at her that's all. She's quite a sensitive soul in her covered up way isn't she? It would kill her if they did. Huh! As for Gerald - he makes me approve of euthanasia; just the thought of him. He always has.' She smiled brightly - her face lit with mischief. 'Do you realize,' she said, 'we'll never have to see him again!' And she stubbed out her cigarette much to Anna's relief.

At the same time and far, far away from them, Pepe sat hunched in a room lit only by a kerosene lamp. Despite the dimness of a lowered flame, the concentration on his face radiated a clear and total involvement with what he did. Immersed and at one with himself, he felt that rare moment of unqualified happiness as he held the objects of his joy. He spat on his black boots - his best - and cleaned them with a cloth. Then with meticulous care, he applied the black polish all over them. He held them close to his eyes while he did this, and inhaled the waxy animal smell that came from the leather. Once finished he waited for them to dry. Then he rubbed them until they shone and he hummed in unison with his arm. Occasionally, he paused and stared at the wall in front of him. The early smiles of triumph hovered beneath his moustache. He waited a while before checking the shine again, then he got to his feet. He wrapped a cloth over the boots and tucked them beneath his arm. He put out the flame, opened the door and stepped out into the street. Immediately the smell of lime trees filled his nostrils, their scent enhanced by the warm and humid night air. He glanced towards the square and beyond; he heard voices, singing and laughter. The sound of a bandoneon tuning up pumped stilted notes into the night. Pepe looked up towards the stars.

'I'm ready.' he whispered.

The Man Who Danced with a Pig
(Concerning Honor)

available from Amazon.

About Sally Campbell

Life for Sally, began in Argentina on a large farm, where she ran wild and free until the age of nine. Her parents decided on an English education. Six years were spent as a boarder followed by one in Switzerland. Then, secretarial college in Cambridge before London for several years of fun and part time jobs. She began writing when she was twenty-six completing two long novels. Twice married with three children, she now lives in Argentina. The constant theme of her writing pursues the chasm between the Latin and Anglo-Saxon mentalities. It is analysed with a subtle eye - at once profound and light-hearted. Her stories reveal a deep familiarity and understanding of this subject.
She has now opened her home in Argentina to writers and those who seek 'wide open spaces, peace and privacy – to think, to write, to be.'

Printed in Great Britain
by Amazon.co.uk, Ltd.,
Marston Gate.